SURVIVAL IN A HOSTILE ENVIRONMENT

WHAT TO DO WHEN YOUR BOSS/ COLLEAGUES WANT YOU DEAD

CHIKA DIOKPALA OSSAI-UGBAH

WestBow
PRESS
A DIVISION OF THOMAS NELSON

WestBow Press books may be ordered through booksellers or by contacting:

WestBow Press
A Division of Thomas Nelson
1663 Liberty Drive
Bloomington, IN 47403
www.westbowpress.com
1-(866) 928-1240

Because of the dynamic nature of the Internet, any Web addresses or links contained in this book may have changed since publication and may no longer be valid. The views expressed in this work are solely those of the author and do not necessarily reflect the views of the publisher, and the publisher hereby disclaims any responsibility for them.

Any people depicted in stock imagery provided by Thinkstock are models, and such images are being used for illustrative purposes only.

Certain stock imagery © Thinkstock.

ISBN 978-1-4497-1068-2 (sc)
ISBN 978-1-4497-1071-2 (dj)
ISBN: 978-1-4497-1069-9 (e)

Library of Congress Control Number: 2010942714

Scripture taken from the New King James Version. Copyright 1979, 1980, 1982 by Thomas Nelson, inc. Used by permission. All rights reserved.

Printed in the United States of America

WestBow Press rev. date: 1/14/2011

FOREWORD

It has always given me great joy and satisfaction to be part of the literary efforts of people with whom I have been associated as co-workers in the Lord's vineyard. This exploratory and innovative publication title: *Survival in A Hostile Environment,* is emerging from a young, dynamic, progressive and unassuming teacher, preacher and scholar. Considering the background of the author, being a brilliant scholar of Hebrew language, he has carefully translated key words from the Hebrew text to the English Language in order to bring out the full meaning of the message.

The book consists of twelve chapter, all of which draw heavily on the Holy Scripture – the Bible. The book deals with various facets of survival in a hostile environment. All the chapters create coherent and interconnected common focus. This makes the reading very appealing to all, that once you start you will not like to drop it until it is completed cover to cover and over again as the word of God gives you greater, deeper meaning and challenges. This no doubt reflects the wide coverage and relevance of the subject in our contemporary society.

The content of the book clearly shows that the author is under the guidance of God Almighty in that this work is not only a labour of love, but also a fountain of words of spiritual inspiration which readers will appreciate as food for spiritual growth.

This book aims and turns out to be a timely write-up of the many demonstrations of his work. This book is interesting for all who desire to survive in a hostile environment even when the enemies want you dead. It is readable, digestible and absorbable.

Deacon Samuel .U. Akpovi.
Associate Professor,
Institute of Public Administration and Extension Services,
University of Benin,
Benin City, Nigeria.

To
Chief Joseph Aninze Ossai-Ugbah
My father, adviser and friend.
Chukwu deme ishi o, makọni okeri abu ẹghọ.

CONTENTS

PREFACE

Bishop Thomas Dexter Jakes, Pastor, Potter's House, has written a classic best seller titled *The Ten Commandments of Working in a Hostile Environment*.[1] In his book Jakes focuses on how you can turn on your passion to achieve your purpose. I do not by any means intend to duplicate the work of the master. In this book of survival in a hostile environment I intend to arm us with 12 disciples of survival. If we are to survive in a hostile environment we should begin by understanding the disciplines and what they are. The main thrust of this book is using the life of David to draw out lessons as necessary companions for survival in every hostile environment.

It would be ideal if no boss, colleague, co-worker or relation were unreasonable, nasty, grabber-grabby, abusive, and offensive or did other troubling and unfair things. But business, life, environments and institutions are not ideal. Certainly, a boss, colleague, co-workers, or board members have their own responsibilities for relationships with others which include us, but this is not a book about what the other person has to do to fulfill us. This is a book about what we can and must do to get along with others in every hostile environment where we find ourselves. We must not just pray as believers in Christ; we must take concrete practical steps to remain overcomers.

The Bible shows David as someone who operated, ministered, lived and worked in a hostile environment. Yet, though He was God's anointed King and could be independent of His environment, he adopted concrete actions to elevate himself beyond the various forms of hostilities. David faced more hostility than could have been imagined. Imagine the pestering servants of Saul envying his role as court musician. Think about the political intrigues of marriage issues, temptations, betrayal by his co-worker and fellow, Doeg, for royal gain. David was a victim of the highest form of human environmental hostility, yet he never lost his focus. He managed to keep his dream alive, identified his hostile antagonists, moved beyond criticism, and survived his circumstances without bitterness and depression. This is exactly what this book passes across.

Chika Diokpala Ossai-Ugbah.
January 2010.

CHAPTER ONE:

OPEN YOUR EYES AND YOUR EARS TO KNOW WHERE YOU ARE.

Now it had happened as they were coming home, when David was returning from the slaughter of the Philistine, that the women had come out of all the cities of Israel, singing and dancing, to meet King Saul, with tambourines, with joy, and with musical instruments.7 So the women sang as they danced, and said: "Saul has slain his thousands, And David his ten thousands." 8 Then Saul was very angry, and the saying displeased him; and he said, "They have ascribed to David ten thousands, and to me they have ascribed only thousands. Now what more can he have but the kingdom?"9 So Saul eyed David from that day forward.10 And it happened on the next day that the distressing spirit from God came upon Saul, and he prophesied inside the house. So David played music with his hand, as at other times; but there was a spear in Saul's hand.11 And Saul cast the spear, for he said, "I will pin David to the wall!" But David escaped his presence twice. (1 Samuel 18: 6 – 11 NKJV).

A hostile environment exists when a person experiences harassment and fears going to work or being in a place because of the offensive, intimidating, or oppressive atmosphere generated by the harasser. When the employer, superior or tutor creates or tolerates a hostile environment directed at you, that person might be trying to force you to quit, compromise, condescend or brake from your principles and patterns of living. Beware. A hostile environment presents itself when unwelcome conduct unreasonably interferes with an individual's academic or work performance *or* creates an intimidating or hostile academic or work environment, even without tangible or economic consequences. The critical inquiry in a hostile environment case is that the conduct is sufficiently "severe or pervasive" to create an abusive academic or work environment. [1]

Most hostile environments include atmosphere of suspicion, uncomplimentary language, unwelcome sexual advances, requests for sexual favors, and other forms of verbal or physically harassing conduct. An atmosphere is hostile when such conducts, actions and attitudes have the purpose or effect of unreasonably interfering with an individual's person, passion, purpose and peace. A hostile environment exists when these unwelcome, unwanted, or offensive conducts interfere with an individual's work or academic performance, or create an intimidating, hostile, or offensive working or learning environment.[2] Unless conduct is egregious, a single or isolated incident of offensive conduct generally does not create a hostile environment. It generally requires a pattern of offensive conduct or offensive language inimical to performance of one's duty or assignment in a place. Similarly, in *quid pro quo* cases, a single incident will only constitute harassment if it is linked to the granting or denial of academic or employment benefits. Harassment carries a bad intent on the part of the harasser.

David was living or rather working in a hostile environment but he did not know it. Saul was troubled with an evil spirit and the mastery of music by David became a soothing balm against the demonic attacks. While David's work was worthwhile, David was considered a threat by Saul. This was because of the supposed praise sung by women when he was returning from the victory over Goliath. Though it was a victory for David, it was indeed a victory for Saul in particular and Israel in general. David was living dangerously because he could not interpret his circumstance. David saw that to survive in a hostile environment, the first key is open your eyes and ears to know where one is. Do not walk with your eyes and ears closed. **Open your eyes and ears to the sights and sounds of where you are.** Do not be like the proverbial Ostrich; do no bury your head in sand. Watch out for causes of a hostile environment.

A hostile environment results from several factors. David found himself in a hostile environment because of the praise of people due to his exploits in the battle field. However, the praise was over and against that of Saul, the King. Saul therefore said if they could ascribe thousands to David and just a thousand to him then, the kingdom was as good as David's. Saul was angry and the saying displeased him. Two things: anger and displeasure created a hostile environment for David. The word "anger" (chârâh-Hebrew) means to *glow or grow warm, to blaze up, wax hot, and become incensed*.[3] Again, Saul was displeased. It also means to be out of tune or express displeasure. The word "displeased" (yâra-Hebrew) is to feel grieved or be broken up emotionally.[4] The hostile environment is among others, a result of inferiority complex. Bosses and colleagues do become threatened and intimidated by one's credentials and also because they can misinterpret a situation.

Every institution, work, living or learning environment has a language of survival; be quick to know it. Be careful to look out for the acceptable language in your business environment. Even your boss or lecturer might not be at home with a language, therefore be careful in your use and acceptance of certain languages, vocabulary and praise. If not it will definitely land you in trouble. It was what people said that brought trouble to David. What people say might be interpreted in any way in your living, learning or work environment by your boss or superior, especially if it hurts their pride. Therefore, be careful of what you say, the jokes you make, the accolades you receive that directly run through your superior.

Sometimes those we work with, live with or learn under are threatened by the things they see and hear about us. Therefore, beware how your praises are sung before your boss. Beware how you also carry your credentials around because you might be just better suited for the job than your boss. Similarly, beware of the complimentary statements made about you in public that might seem to cross the path of your boss.

Some of our bosses and superiors have emotional problems, some with very serious psychosomatic disorder, some are battling with a split personality, some are trailed with inferiority complex, some have postpartum depression and some others are emotionally repressed. Watch out to know where you are and who you work with. Those with personality conflicts or disability can easily lay anything they consider threatening to heart and would use it against you. Learn to understand the kind of person you are relating with.

Do not be an object of retaliation. David was suffering for the depression Saul faced for disobedience. Do not position yourself between two bosses at war. Retaliation might also be a cause for a hostile environment.[5] Retaliation because your boss hurt another boss and you unknowingly took sides through your conduct. Retaliation might also come because you failed to give due credit to the supposed ingenuity of your boss. When you are exalted for a job in your department or school as a member of staff, be quick to point to the role of your boss in helping to make that achievement possible.

Do not do things or engage in things that will hurt the pride or ego of your boss. Be wise to play the safe game. When you notice that you have a better propensity for the job or that you are more knowledgeable than your superior in a field, do not cross his path with your intelligence. Do not openly confront his ignorance. Discrimination due to potential, race, sex and colour can also be a cause for hostile environment.

Do not call attention or attraction to yourself. Undue attraction and attention you call to yourself, your achievement, potential, beauty, sex, figure and person can bring you a hostile environment. Learn to maintain a low profile sometimes, no matter who you are and what you have. Some of us have been able to achieve what our bosses or superiors have not been able to do or took several years of toil and struggle to achieve. Some of these superiors and bosses were not able to go to school on time; at your age they were still roaming around without hope until destiny smiled on them. When they see you with your age, position and attainment some feel really upset and infuriated. Learn not to *zoom* your car around with braggadocio, especially if your car is bigger and better than that of your boss or superior.[6] If you do, you are finished. One of my respected advisers, Mr. J. O. Ehima, J.P., member institute of Chartered Accountants of Nigeria (ICAN), decided to go for a Masters in Business Administration in one of our universities in Nigeria. As a respected fellow of the institute of Chartered Accountants of Nigeria (ICAN), he was abreast with most of the course content. In fact, his course mates called him "professor." One of the courses on tax administration, which was particularly his field, he came across the textbook that the lecturer used as his personal note from which he dictated his assumed notes word for word. Mr. Ehima not only showed it to the class, but was unfortunate enough to have been singled out by the class as a chartered fellow. In the examination that followed, the lecturer scored him a "c" grade. All attempts to recall his script for remarking failed as it was never found. If attention, had not called to who he was, what several persons who are facing hostilities due the way they vaunt their sex physique. Beware!

Most of the time, we are censored and cornered in a hostile environment because we are oblivious of the signs. People become aware of a "hostile environment" based on a few isolated incidents of objectionable conduct or comments, but it can be more than these. Generally speaking, if only a few isolated incidents have occurred, and if those incidents are not too severe, you just begin to get a hint that you are in a hostile environment. It is important to be aware of the environment in which we live, work or study so that we can adequately respond to it. Certain characteristics of a hostile environment are also revealed in suspicion and outright aggression. From the moment Saul heard those praise songs he became suspicious of David. The term "suspicion" (âvan-Hebrew) means to *watch* with jealousy or an evil eye.[7] That would have brought about a reduction in the level of contact and relationship too. Above all, Saul tried to nail David, in fact to kill him. These two actions show us some manifestations of a hostile environment.

Saul wanted to nail David. This is a form of offensive conduct. Sometimes when managers or co-workers are engaging in offensive conduct toward one, the focus is on the traditional protected categories of sex or gender, pregnancy, age, disability, religion, race, or national origin. For example, offensive conduct is occurring in the workplace and the conduct has an element of sexual harassment to it (touching, crude sexual jokes or comments, or otherwise offensive gender-related comments).[8] If someone makes discriminatory comments, or engages in any form of conduct, which is offensive based on sex, gender, pregnancy, age, disability, religion, race, or national origin, if someone's comments or conduct focuses on "pregnancy" or "age" or "disability" or "religion" or "race" or "national origin," then this is a discriminatory hostile environment situation. The most common is probably racial or sexual harassment.

We can be sexually nailed or intimidated. In a sexually hostile environment, we might have been grabbed or touched in sensitive private areas, or someone keeps rubbing up against you or touching us, or someone has threatened our job if we will not have relationship with them, or someone is making offensive sexual comments to us or about us or in our presence.

We can be verbally nailed. In a hostile environment based on race or age or disability or religion or national origin, we might be subjected to slurs and insults and offensive jokes and comments. Also we sometimes find in a hostile environment a form of bad conduct toward us if a boss or colleague has a motive to retaliate. In some other occasion, it might just be simply generic rudeness or disrespect or unfairness.

We might be ethnically or religiously nailed. This is a special problem: Sometimes in a particular work environment, coloured or women are simply treated worse than whites or men. In Nigeria every tribe cries out over marginalization, but who is marginalizing who? We are marginalizing ourselves. So, in a typical government institution in Edo land for instance, one is expected to "Edolize" or else get out of favour. We will also notice that in such places even in serious meetings of department heads, the local dialect takes center stage instead of English.

We can be religiously nailed. Most times complaints and gossips against us are not about productivity but about our religion. This is especially the case if our religion, Christianity has helped one display open integrity and forthrightness that has not made some persons to dance around with undeserved monetary provisions in the institution.

We can be officially nailed with ease in the form of queries that are filed and not disposed off. Any form of bad conduct toward you is suspicious if the boss is trying to make you quit or weaken your chances of promotion. Such bad conduct, come in written form of warnings that is documented.

This is because our boss might be trying to gain an advantage in an anticipated legal dispute or administrative action with us. For example, the boss might desire to send one away but he does not want to part with certain entitlements, so the boss attempts to build a file against one to show that one deserved to be fired, or the boss tries to get one to resign. Either way, the goal is to weaken our ability to enforce our contract, or weaken our defenses against the organization. Watch out for what causes a hostile environment and walk in God's divine presence to survive.

CHAPTER TWO:

WALK IN GOD'S DIVINE PRESENCE.

Now Saul was afraid of David, because the LORD was with him, but had departed from Saul.13 Therefore Saul removed him from his presence, and made him his captain over a thousand; and he went out and came in before the people.14 And David behaved wisely in all his ways, and the LORD was with him.15 Therefore, when Saul saw that he behaved very wisely, he was afraid of him.16 But all Israel and Judah loved David, because he went out and came in before them. (1 Samuel 18: 12 – 16 NKJV).

The work, living or learning environment is supposed to be civilized, tolerant and supportive. It's tough enough to come in each day to earn your daily bread or learn for progress without things getting nasty after you arrive. When all seems to be going along smoothly in strict accord with responsible conduct, it is easy to start taking things for granted. Unless you are one of the few who are lucky enough to have kind-hearted and supportive bosses or professors, most of your working or learning life would probably be spent trying to survive the workplace.

Some experiences in a hostile environment include: harassment, fears of going to work or being in a place because of the offensive, intimidating, or oppressive atmosphere generated by the harasser.[1] There are also bottled up emotions among employees or students and creativity is stifled in such an environment. Most persons living, working or learning in a hostile environment experience migraines, high blood pressure and even heart attacks.

In a hostile environment incompetent and difficult individuals create a lot of stress and frustration at workplaces or school. Unfortunately for most of us, such people turn out to be our bosses or professors. It is a known fact that persons with inferiority complex and low self esteem do sometimes end up in high positions and in the hierarchy of power just like Saul. Are you caught up in a hostile environment? Are you struggling with your job? Are you troubled with your career and, like David, your boss is afraid of you? Saul subjected David to stress and frustration because the Lord departed from him and was with David. You might be subjected to the low grades, taunts, verbal assaults, systemic deprivation, discrimination and others because your boss notices a special favour around you. How do you survive such times? It is to walk in God's divine presence like David. The secret of David's survival is anchored in the statement "The Lord was with him". In other words, David walked and lived in God' divine presence.

How do we stay in the presence of God during work or school in such a hostile environment? There is something we can do when we get caught up in the politics, hidden agenda, or personality wars at school or work.

To walk and live in the presence of God means to become actually conscious of God being as present. It is a simple act which involves the impression of the unseen Being with whom we have immediate relation and familiar conversation, whose goodness towards us is assured, and who loves us with an everlasting love; who exercises a particular providence among us, who is present everywhere and "who is heart-reading, heart-changing, ever accessible and open to penetration," according to Cardinal Newman.[2] We should walk in His divine presence. How can we walk and live in God's divine presence?

Prayer as divine watch and wait plays a crucial part in walking in God's divine presence. If ever there was a time when we needed prayer, now is that time. Think of the stress you face at work or school, the frustrations of your promotions, the sexual hunts and demands, the discrimination you face in sharing of favours, the undue verbal assaults and even the threats to your life and progress. For our faith to have meaning and power in these times of job stress and learning chaos, we must practice the discipline of prayer.

Prayer is the essential key to connect us to God. Prayer draws God near to us in that it draws us closer to the source of our life. Prayer ties us to every human being throughout time. Prayer possesses the power to create new energy in you to help you cope with the pressures and challenges at work or school. Prayer can change the course of life from career death, educational frustration and developmental hindrances. The Scriptures are filled with episodes where prayer transformed incredible situations into unbelievable opportunities. It is rather unfortunate to observe that some of us think prayer is a weak substitute for strategic action. We may feel prayer is what you do when you can do nothing else. Know that we can do nothing without prayer. It is the greatest offering you can offer yourself in your pain of job frustration, desperation for career intervention and abandonment by those in the corridors of power. There is nothing within our grasp that can be achieved without prayer. I am a living witness that prayer works.

Whenever and wherever efforts are forged to divide your provision and wage war against your success or progress, you should be driven to declare God's will in prayer. In prayer we remind the powers-that-be that we are divinely ordained to live in peace, prosper in the things you lay your hands to do, live as God's king and priest. In prayer we remind the forces and factors at play in our place of work that no one can take our place.

In prayer we draw upon the power of the supernatural for wisdom to succeed at work, for revelation of the counsels of evil and how you should conduct your self the next day. Never go to work or school or confront any hostile environment without having allowed prayer to saturate your day. Prayer is the trumpet of victory that alerts the powers to the independence and coronation of the child of God. In order to have courage to take bold decisions, reject unpopular advances, and strategically survive a negative plot, you need a well-developed practise of prayer. Prayer makes the difference between deliverance and disaster. Think of those feelings of dread that haunt your heart, the dreams where your hands are chained at work, your file is mutilated, your credentials are stolen or cancelled, your boss dressed in black or red clothing and chanting incantations over you, or your boss subjects you to punishment or physical abuse, it is then a time to pray.

In prayer we are on a collision course with unthinkable factors and forces. We need prayer. The divine Presence is what prayer brings. Prayer releases heaven into your soul. In prayer we report our harassers to heaven. Everything else about prayer revolves around divine Presence, seeking it in depths dark or luminous - rejoicing in it, delighting in this or that aspect of the Presence, imploring its help, begging redemptive forgiveness from a God present to my guilt and to my remorse. Being drawn to the Presence is a gift from God. A member of my congregation, Baba W. Mokogwu, was Director of Library services in Delta State. He had a difficult board chairman who called himself *Lucifer* and who created a hostile work environment for him. Baba discovered that, as he prayed before every board meeting, the Lord would reveal to him the nature of each meeting. That was how he was able to overcome the self-styled "Lucifer".

Proclamation of the word is also indispensable. We have to know that though we are in a hostile environment, there is a mind of heaven about us. If in prayer we attack the forces and factors around our job, in proclamation we prophesy into our lives. The announcement is based on the prophetic capsules heaven has made available to you through the speaking of the word. There is nowhere that the word of the Lord is exposed that heaven does not leave an invitation for someone. No doubt there is a promise about your future and your job. There was something that God said before you took up that appointment; there was a word he dropped in your spirit about your assignment; there was a specific saying that heaven called your attention to. That is the word that keeps you in divine presence as you work or learn in a hostile environment.

Believe in yourself as you go to work or school. Bless your work, those we would meet and relate with, even that difficult boss or lecturer. Stop cursing the day and work. Do not pray to avoid your boss or not to be seen by them; rather speak to your day to use them to bless you. It does not matter if for 20 years, 10 years or whatever, they have never seen to your good. Heaven still believes in you. Therefore, believe in yourself: No matter how bad the situation around you seems, do not lose hope. You have to have faith in yourself and keep your mind frames in a positive mode. Replace negative, inappropriate reactions with different, more acceptable ones. Even though the job or environment is negative, change it through your active confession. It is up to you to specify exactly what is and should be in your hostile environment.

Similarly centered on our proclamation is a passion to bless the difficult environment we find ourself working or learning in. In this act of blessing, speak to the factors and forces in control for release of joy and expectations. Carry a language of heaven on your lips even towards those who harass and intimidate you, and deprive you of your due promotions. The other thing in this regard is, focus on each person used to create the hostile environment and in your mind say "God bless you..." This helps to turn on your peace, joy and good side.

There is a relationship between the words you say about someone and your emotional disposition towards the individual. The more joyful and peaceful we are at work, school or in meetings, the more our mind becomes "expansive" and willing to discover and accept many possibilities and many diverse opinions. Also the more likely we are to complain, the more we have feelings of anger or anxiety, the more close-minded we become and we listen with the narrow intention of advocating for our agenda, which has less desirable results. Instill positive attitudes in yourself and in others. Be the role model for those who feel like quitting. You can prevent their negativity by instilling in them the positivist bug. If you do that, they may never catch the negativity virus again. Sure, you can leave your worries behind at your desk and go home with a smile on your face. But that smile can last long only when you do not allow an abusive boss strip away your dignity and pride. Restore your self-esteem and self-worth through what you say to yourself.

Praise is an instrument that turns trials into testimony. Praising God makes every circumstance of our lives complete, essential, and eminently worthwhile. To praise is to admire, commend, extol, honor, and worship. It is *the joyful thanking and adoring of the Lord and the celebration of His goodness and grace.* Psalm 22:3 informs us, "But you are Holy, enthroned on the praises of Israel." The Hebrew word for enthroned is *yawshab* and it means to remain, to settle, or marry! When we praise God, His presence comes and settles upon us! His kingdom power and glory manifest wherever God dwells or "settles." And there is joy IN HIS PRESENCE! That's the reason we renew our strength when we take the time to wait on God or to spend time in praise and worship. Satan has already been defeated by the Lord Jesus and we share His victory over the forces of darkness. When we begin to praise and worship God, we enforce victory over that defeat in our current situation. Your enemies have to back out in their schemes to hinder us! Praise helps you to function best within divine guidelines and creates an ideal environment.

Praising God in a hostile environment or in difficult situations releases His delivering power over our enemy! Several of us face 'giants' at work or school. The hostile environment in which we live, work or learn causes us depression, grief, abuse, frustration, fear, emotional hurt and anger. Some of us struggle with the discouragement of career breakdown, promotion issues, or experience anxiety over employment/work or lack thereof. Some others are wrestling with issues of sexual harassment and verbal abuse. We all desire to be free from these challenges and pains everyday since we have to face our hostile environment. Beloved, keep your song near you. Put on your garment of praise instead of a spirit of despair!

Praise is an expression of faith, and a declaration of victory! It declares that we believe God is with us and is in control of the outcome of all our circumstances. You might have been physically threatened, abused and violated, but keep a song on your lips. As you go to work, learn or live in your hostile environment, do not throw away your song. Keep your songs coming. Praise will keep you celebrated. It will put smile on your lips, courage in your spirit and strength into your body. Praise is the "gate-pass" which allows us to enter the sacredness of His glory. Praise elevates us into God's Presence and power. Praise means "to commend, to applaud or magnify." For the Christian, praise to God is an expression of worship in spite of the circumstance. Praise is the secret of how to lift your hearts above your troubles and enter into God's presence and power. Through praise and worship your heart is raised into the joyous presence and peace of God. It provides God a channel for His power to operate in your circumstances. Keep your song near you.

In a hostile environment, praise transports you into the realm of the supernatural and into the power of God. I want you to know that praise is a delivery system through which you inject scripture internally into your spirit. Praise helps to attack the enemy of doubt, fear, frustration, anger and retaliation in a hostile environment. That is why the praise I am talking about is vertical praise. In vertical praise, we minister to God and He in turn grants us release. In vertical praise we focus on God and not on our pains.

Praise sends the enemy running. In a hostile environment, praise makes you unpredictably positive. You might be subjected to pains and every arsenal in the harassers' possession is thrown at you, but when you praise and keep praising God, the creators of a hostile environment get confused and confounded. They begin to wonder: "in spite of all I have done to frustrate this man or woman, in spite of the programmed discrimination from favour, he or she has remained joyous". Since praise manifests God's presence, also realize that praise repels the presence of the enemy. Praise creates an atmosphere of power. An atmosphere which is filled with sincere worship and praise to God by humble and contrite hearts is disgusting to the Devil. He fears the power in the name of Jesus, in our praise he flees from the Lord's habitation. *"Whoever offers praise glorifies me; And to him who orders his conduct aright I will show the salvation of God" (Psalms 50:23).*

CHAPTER THREE

WATCH THE FAVOURS YOU RECEIVE.

Then Saul said to David, "Here is my older daughter Merab; I will give her to you as a wife. Only be valiant for me, and fight the LORD'S battles." For Saul thought, "Let my hand not be against him, but let the hand of the Philistines be against him."18 So David said to Saul, "Who am I, and what is my life or my father's family in Israel, that I should be son-in-law to the king?"19 But it happened at the time when Merab, Saul's daughter, should have been given to David, that she was given to Adriel. 20 Now Michal, Saul's daughter, loved David. And they told Saul, and the thing pleased him.21 So Saul said, "I will give her to him, that she may be a snare to him, and that the hand of the Philistines may be against him." Therefore Saul said to David a second time, "You shall be my son-in-law today."22 And Saul commanded his servants, "Communicate with David secretly, and say, 'Look, the king has delight in you, and all his servants love you. Now therefore, become the king's son-in-law.'"23 So Saul's servants spoke those words in the hearing of David. And David said, "Does it seem to you a light thing to be a king's son-in-law, seeing I am a poor and lightly esteemed man?"24 And the servants of Saul told him, saying, "In this manner David spoke."25 Then Saul said, "Thus you shall say to David: 'The king does not desire any dowry but one hundred foreskins of the Philistines, to take vengeance on the king's enemies.'" But Saul thought to make David fall by the hand of the Philistines.26 So when his servants told David these words, it pleased David well to become the king's son-in-law. Now the days had not expired. (1 Samuel 18: 17 – 29 NKJV).

Work and learning should be fun and not stress. However, we are witnesses to the fact that several persons are under torment due to their learning, living or work environment which has become hostile. This hostile environment is by no means natural; rather it is created by some factors and persons. For some of us a difficult work or learning environment is created by a difficult boss, or, as many people say, "a crazy boss." Some of these bosses are bullies, while some others can also be belittling, burned-out, controlling, insecure, micromanaging, namby-pamby, or paranoid. Some are always aggressive; some do not listen or continually reject or hijack your ideas; some are critical, impatient, and always feel superior. The real question is, what kind of boss do you face when you get to work or school? And what can you do about him or her or about the situation?

In a hostile work or learning environment, a boss's attitude may make completing even the simplest tasks difficult. In this section we shall again focus on the life of David to draw inspiration from him. You have to know that when you are in a hostile environment, the harasser would stop at nothing to get you fired, dent your record and weave you into a mesh of trouble. One tactic which the harasser adopts is to try to show you act of favour. This act of favour might be like pushing you into the main stream of administrative and executive responsibilities, giving you assignments that seem to expose you, to bring out your best, presenting you with gifts of outstanding qualities, privileges and even opportunities as it were for you to showcase your skill and potential. Do not be carried away to believe that your harasser is extending the olive branch to you.

When you begin to receive serious attention of unsolicited favours from your harasser, be careful: he or she might have adopted another game plan. This was the strategy of King Saul. When Saul saw that he could not deal with David, still intimidated by David, he adopted the strategy of giving a wife to David. It would be a great honour to be the Son in-law of the King, but David was weary of the offer. Saul's purpose for the favour of marriage to David was to destroy him. To survive in a hostile environment, you must **watch the favours you receive**. Be very careful how you handle and accept such favours so that you can last long where you are and fulfill your destiny. So when unsolicited favours begin to come from your harasser, watch out.

Match the favour of your harasser with your person. Saul made an important advance to David when things had gone out of hand. It actually appeared now as if he was interested in the welfare and growth of David, but was he? He approached David to make him a Son-in-law by marrying his daughter, Merab. Saul felt that since he could not deal with David personally, he could use the circumstance surrounding the favour to work against David and lead him to his down fall. What Saul wanted as dowry was simple, 100 armour coats of killed Philistine soldiers. Saul wanted David to die by the hands of the Philistines.

David matched the favour with his person. He considered his person, family background, and credentials and therefore hesitated in accepting the offer. There are some of us who forget who we are as we strive to gather and collect every favour that comes our way. We have to know that some favours are beyond us. Your boss might want to dominate and cage you through marriage, a relationship, and enlistment into a social club or organization. Please beware. Try to ask yourself certain questions, does this favour agree with who I am? Does it fit into my personality? Does it fit into my character, attitude, likes and dislikes? When you betray your personality for official gain, you lose your personal identity and respect. Your personality is your distinctive colour.

There is something about every person that makes him or her unique. You may not believe that, but it is true. It is a useful idea to hold as you try to find your mission in life even under threat and harassment. Holding that idea of who you are and what you want will help you go through those harassments and still feel great. The perfect career for you must be something you like to do even in the midst of uncertainty. It should be something worthwhile; in fact, something needed and wanted in the world. If you do not like to do your work, you would not be happy, even when you are off work. Also, not only that, you are not likely to work hard enough at it to succeed and conquer the odds against you. And if your work is not worthwhile, it will feel as though life were empty and had no meaning. So, do not sell your soul for official favours that do not give your life meaning. Any compromise of your personality is in the inroad to the destruction of your life's mission. Where you have no sense of mission, your life is a *miss-take*.

People who are parents under harassment often find ready-made purpose in life because of the importance human beings place on the rearing of children. Sure, continuation of the species is important, but biological reproduction is not such a big accomplishment. And when children grow up, parents speak of the "empty nest syndrome," and end up facing many of the same challenges as everyone else. Rather than adding more people to an already-crowded planet in bid to let off steam, there are many other ways to hold on to our dreams. Even in your hostile environment, volunteering your time with extra job demands can give your life value. Choose professional paths that put your natural instincts to work in other ways. You can help make your work, or hostile environment, a better place through your contribution and creativity. Others find that participating in the natural world – gardening, environmental awareness – fulfills their yearning to make things better. Pay attention to what is going on around you right now. What clues do you find to what makes you happy? You are in touch with your passion when you do something just because you love it, not because you are especially good at it, or other people tell you that you should do it or because you make a lot of money when you do it. Fun is the fuel that life runs on. How full is your tank?

To find meaning in the midst of your harassment, look into the activities of your life and see how much of your activities follow a single theme or particular trend. Therein may lie where life holds its meaning for you. Whatever you find as a theme common to the times you are happy and harassed, you can assume it is the direction of your mission in life. It is in a direction that is right for you. Now put more of it in your life. Gradually add more of it, maybe an hour of it every week for the next month or two. Then make it two hours a week. Keep adding more, pursuing your interest. The whole tone of your life will rise, and you will be happier and rise above the limitation factors and forces of hostile harassments.

Meaning is an interest in life's purpose which is sometimes beyond us. Some of us suffer from a sort of low-grade depression because we do not find meaning in life. Our work is all about money and not about our happiness and fulfillment. Many of us may not actually be hurting, but we are pretty disinterested or disconnected. What is going on, and what can we do about it? Finding the juice in your life is important if you want to be truly happy. Your happiness should not be dictated by the environmental indices of external attacks, rather, it should be from the passion that you pursue in a place. That passion is what determines your pulse and eventually results in success or failure.

Again, in watching the favours you receive; match the favour with your pulse. By this I mean, are you under pressure to accept an offer or a compromise or something? Saul was really intent on making David accept the favour of being his son-in-law. Therefore to hatch his plot of destroying David, he presented Micah, another daughter of his, to marry David. This time around, he might have studied Micah's character and believed she could do the job. Saul wanted Micah to be a snare to David. The word snare, *mokesh* in Hebrew, means bait for catching a bird or a fish.[1] Still within this snare was the desire of Saul to get David eliminated through the hands of the Philistines.

Beware, all that glitter is not gold. When you notice that pressure is mounted on you to accept certain favours directly or indirectly, something sinister might be up somewhere. When your harasser wants to achieve a goal and it is not being achieved, be aware that they will mount pressure on you. This can be done through making things difficult for you, making achieving even the basic things in your work or school stressful. The harasser can use those around you to consistently speak to you about the issue, presenting things, issues and events that make your coming into contact with accepting the offer easy or tempting. Beware!

But there are some breakthroughs that lead to heart break; there are some favours that breed frustration; there are some gifts that are gambling, and there are some offers that are offences. The path to career destruction, demotion and even crisis that some persons face is in accepting opportunities provided by your harassers that appear to give them paths to greatness. Do not accept favours that will open your back door. When favours become baits, you are really vulnerable because you have not closed your back door. Think; think very well when your harasser invites you to a dinner, a birthday bash, an obituary outing or a luncheon.

Consider emotional, psychological, spiritual and lifestyle pressures that can get you stuck as you seek to find and fulfill your mission in life. You can assess if any of these "calling blockers" are hindering you in discerning or living out your happiness. Your pulse provides you with "calling catalysts" you can utilize to conquer your official blockers. Motivate yourself to take action against your pressures. Learning how to take appropriate action is a key part of becoming the person you so desire to be. When you do, you would have used the opportunity to make personal mission statements, set boundaries and colour your life. It is an action plan that would later determine how far you can go on to live your life in spite of the harassments against you. Learn how to live your calling successfully. Your life matters. Many people are inspired to pursue their passion; fewer persevere to live it faithfully over the course of their lives because their pulse rates drop. You can create a vital support system for yourself through your potential to enable you to fulfill the mission that is yours alone.

Match the favour of your harassers with your potential. Furthermore, Saul went ahead to press the issue to David. What David did again is commendable; he matched the favour with his potential. Saul named his dowry that was the deal for the offer. David knew it was what he could do and he therefore went ahead to complete the process. Some favours are beyond your potential and are meant to display your stupidity and ignorance: do not give your harasser an opportunity to place you in an embarrassing position. Make sure you are capable before accepting an offer.

So, when such unsolicited favours come from your harasser, focus on your potential. Begin by making a complete and accurate assessment of your potential. To do this you must take an inventory of yourself. You will make a few lists. Sit down and make a list of all the things you can do well.

Be honest with yourself. When that list is done, make a list of all the things you like to do, even if you think you cannot do them well. Then, make a list of all the things you would like to do, if you could. Then, go back to the list of things you can do well. You are probably being too simple; ask trusted friends to assess you.

A voice within you might be saying "You are so dumb," or "You cannot learn to do that," or "You never do anything right," or similar nasty things. Shut off that voice - you can do it - and add a few more things to the list of things you can do well. Pretend you are your best friend - it's amazing how much more forgiving and charitable we are with our friends than we are with ourselves. Now that you are your best friend, you should be able to add a few more items to your "do well" list. But do be honest - don't list things you feel you really can't do well.

Next, go to your list of things you would like to do if you could. Ask yourself, "Why cannot I do this, if I would like to?" Put your reasons on another list. So you have a lot of lists going - what good is that going to do? Well, you have just made an assessment of yourself. Focus on what you can do - focus on your potential. Make it a habit to focus on your strengths. Do not forget to include your undeveloped potential as well.

Train yourself to focus on your potential instead of your limitations. Focusing on your strengths lets you make the decision. You will do well, because you will be doing what you really want to do and you will be determined to develop the full potential of your strengths. Very few people concentrate on fully developing any of their strengths. That's where you will have the edge. You know your true disadvantages, but your determination, your singleness of purpose, will inspire you to fully develop the talents and skills you do have. Beloved, you can survive any hostile environment if you watch the favours you receive. Do not be caught unawares and cheaply too. Be on guard.

Have you ever thought about it that you are not in this world by accident? Your life definitely counts for God and for humanity. So, think deeply: what did you want to be when you grew up or what do you want to be that you are not yet? What unique experience can you still recall in the course of your life's journey in this world? Do you still believe deep down within you that your life has a meaning? That, beyond day dreaming, paper visions and writings, your existence in this world has a mission that no one else can fulfill. Thus your everyday experiences bring you towards the fulfillment of your mission in life.

Winners are people of destiny with a goal. David had an opportunity to tap into his deep everyday experiences and he did. Winners are persons who discover what their life is for and use it for the benefit of total humanity. David saw a similarity between what Saul had promised and what had taken place in the wilderness in the battle with Goliath. He knew he had something to contribute, and he did just that. Except you discover who you are, what you have and who is behind you, your life will count for nothing. So, what do winners discover about their lives that make them winners?.

David knew that he was not in the hostile environment by accident; there was a providential arrangement for him to achieve his mission in life. Your mission is what you live to achieve. The footsteps you leave in the sands of time. When people's hearts were scheming evil, David rose to the challenge because he knew exactly what his mission in life was. It was to be a warrior that would bring liberation to others. Socrates rightly said, "Man, know yourself." Unless you know what you are living for, you do not know yourself. Have you ever taken time to ask yourself, what do I live to achieve in life? If not, your life is a waste. You are only occupying space.

Many people seem to be under the impression that their life's mission, once they discover it, is going to be a particular goal or job or accomplishment that will be an easy road. The mission of your life is not some specific objective you must try to accomplish. The mission of your life is an idea. It is, in fact, the highest ideal that you stand for, and it permeates every single aspect of your life. Whatever your life's mission is, rest assured that you are already living it, at least to some extent. You were guided by it through your childhood, you have used it in making major decisions throughout your life, and you feel its call on a day-to-day basis even now. But the joys you experience sporadically when your mission happens to intersect your daily life are nothing compared to the joy of knowing your mission and creating your life around that purpose in an intentional way.

Pursuing a career, raising a family, devotion to a creative vocation or to a cause, and acquiring property are perhaps the most widespread of long-term missions that make life meaningful, according to such philosophies. One of the interesting things about finding your purpose is that no one else can find it for you. Maybe your parents or the preacher at your childhood church tried to give you answers, and maybe those worked for a while. Ultimately, however, success in life depends on you leading your life the way you choose to do it. Slow down. Give yourself a break from multitasking pressures. Take a deep breath and relax. Life does not become more meaningful if you simply fill it up with more busy-ness. Try doing less, and allow yourself to appreciate completing something you do well. If your life ended tomorrow, what would you want to have accomplished that you have not yet done? It's probably not just spending more time at the office. How would you like your epitaph to read? What do you want your legacy to be? How do you discover meaningful purposes for your life; and once discovered, how do you live purposefully so you can accomplish them? Distraction is one obstacle to a purposeful life. The other is a desire for comfort or pleasant feelings. Both lead us away from a life which offers fulfillment and meaning - a life we can look back on without regrets. According to Pablo Picasso "My mother said to me, If you become a soldier, you will be a general; if you become a monk, you will end up as the Pope." Instead, I became a painter and wound up as Picasso."[2] Richard Leider says "We are born purpose-seeking creatures. Purpose is necessary for our very health and survival. If you doubt this, check out the rates of illness and death when people lose or give up their sense of purpose."[3] One reason people lose their sense of purpose is because they have a limited level of tolerance. Tolerance can and does make you a winner anywhere.

CHAPTER FOUR:

EXPAND YOUR LEVEL OF TOLERANCE

Then the princes of the Philistines went out to war. And so it was, whenever they went out, that David behaved more wisely than all the servants of Saul, so that his name became highly esteemed. (1 Samuel 18: 30 NKJV).

When people work together in groups, there are bound to be individuals who are disagreeable in nature, conflict creators in character, and assassins in their quest for position and placement in the workplace. Whether these people's activities become full-blown or not, they create a hostile environment which feud and fuel problems in people's lives. Therefore, colleagues in our living, learning and work environment can be instrumental in creating a hostile environment.

At any situation of work or learning, we rely on and spend more time with our colleagues than with most other people in our lives: yet we frequently experience conflict at work. Such conflicts range from office or school gossip to outright bullying. In nearly every office or institution there are and will always be personality clashes at some point, and most times they are easily sorted out. However, sometimes they are not sufficiently dealt with, leaving someone with no other option than to resign. One serious problem facing most of us is that, when we find ourselves facing a hostile environment due to difficult colleagues, we lack the ability to Increase our capacity to work with those difficult personalities as David did. Too often we only try to fit in and connect with others similar to us.

In the text above, war continued between the Israelites and the Philistines. David had been appointed commander over the army of Israel. He was to lead to battle a group whom he did not really trust, a group who were not dedicated and committed to his cause and welfare. Can he not be killed by one of his own men in the cause of war and his death seen as a case of mistake of another soldier? To survive, David behaved himself more wisely than all the servants of Saul. The term "behave wisely" means to make or act with prudence, skill or intelligence. The word also means to be circumspect, understanding, to give attention to, consider thoroughly, and have an insight into something. The Hebrew word śâkal describes an action of crossing hands while watching an unfolding situation. However, it is not an attitude of despair but one of insight. So, another key for survival in a hostile environment is to **expand your level of toleration with others**. When you expand your level of tolerance, you increase your ability to be able to work and cope with all kinds of attitudes and yet remain productive. How then can we expand our level of toleration?

Manage your approach with wisdom. Learn how to improve your work environment in spite of difficult people. Things would be fine if your co-workers were as reasonable and affable as you are. Unfortunately, that expectation is a bit too idealistic to have any traction at all. You have to take them as they come, so you might as well get comfortable doing so.

To manage our attitude with wisdom we just have to come out of our shells to understand the kind of people we live, work or learn with and why they behave the way they do. Sometimes as Christians we live in a supposed spiritual castle where all we do is pray to over-turn our situations without seeking to understand why and how they are that way. Beloved, do you really know the character of people you live, learn or work with? There are several categories of unpleasant people: the dominator: outwardly aggressive, the snipers: back stabbers; the graveyard people: always silent, the "notice me"; the "I know it all": the princess; the baby: never grows up and negative; the negators; people pleasers, uncommitted and non-players. The objective is not to change the traits these people display. The idea is to have the tools that can prevent anyone from hindering your journey up the corporate ladder. There are various kinds of people around. An adequate knowledge of personality types helps in the manner of approach that leads to survival. Some of these personalities are pointed out.[1]

The dominators: These hardcore personalities are hostile. They are abusive and intimidating. They always have to be right and will charge like angry bulls if you challenge or cross them. Take a deep breath. Let them blow off steam and express their anger and frustration. But, draw the line. Do not let them get abusive. Address them by name or position to maintain control. Then state your position clearly and avoid the temptation to argue. You will not win a battle with them, especially in a public forum. Learn to set your boundary early on. In fact, know your limit.

The "I know it all": These ones are princes and princesses, self styled experts and appear to know more than others about a particular subject. Those who behave this way are usually computer programmers, lawyers, Judges, accountants and mathematicians. Facts are power to them and since they know the facts, they feel superior. They want to be special and have the center stage. Because you cannot "fake it" with them, make sure you know the facts and information. You can also capitalize on what they know by asking questions. They love to show off and have others appreciate their knowledge. Use their knowledge strategically. Give them praise and maybe they will come down from their towers.

The Snipers: These ones are passive, yet aggressive personality types who take cheap shots at their targets. They undercut your authority in devious ways by using sarcasm, which they often disguise as a joke. They will not be direct with their criticism. Try to turn their attention and comments to the issues, not the personalities involved. Once they realize that you would not put up with their sniping, they usually stop. They do not like to take the center stage and also tend to avoid open confrontation.

The Baby: Babies see everything negatively. They complain, whine, and act defeated. Since they often believe no one thinks they are important, start your interactions by listening to what they say. Steer them toward the facts, which are usually much less negative than what they believe. Maintain control by bringing up the negatives yourself. Then dismiss the negatives logically. Direct the baby's attention to the more positive aspects of the situation. When a baby asks a negative question, turn to the rest of the group to answer. Do not give them much eye contact.

The Negators: Babies seem pale compared to the "negators". Negative persons are not just negative, they distrust anyone in power. They believe that their way is the only right way and their motto is "I told you so." They only and usually see the down side of every issue. Stay positive, but realistic. Delay discussing solutions since Ned or Nancy will dismiss every solution as you bring it up. Refuse to argue with them and stick with the facts.

People pleaser: While these people are easy to like, they can be difficult personalities to deal with. They over-commit themselves and their staff because they cannot say "NO." Carefully limit how much you ask of them to eliminate the disappointments caused by missed deadlines. In meetings, they may tend to volunteer to do much of office work. Try: "You're working on so many worthy projects….who else would like to sign up for this one?" Affirm their contributions and help them say "no."

The Graveyard people: These people are the most difficult personalities to deal with. They do not reveal their true motives, and you end up in a guessing game trying to find out what makes them tick. It is vital to get them to participate in meetings, so they do not leave with their hidden agenda and work counter to the team. The most effective strategy is to draw them out with open-ended questions. Even if the silence between you and this unresponsive person grows chasm-like, wait it out.

The uncommitted: An Uncommitted does not take her job seriously, making her teammates' work more difficult. Work is a very low priority for him or her. For such people, the focus at work is trying to do as little as possible so as to find time to take care of personal matters or other interests. They sense no urgency in getting the work done. Their favorite saying is "It can wait."

Manage your attitude with wisdom. What is attitude? On the surface, it could be described as the disposition we display to others. Elwood N. Chapman claims, "Attitude is a mind set. It is the way you look at things mentally. It is the outward manifestation of a mind that dwells primarily on positive matters."[2] Believe it or not, attitude is contagious. A positive attitude gives energy to you and to those around you. On the other hand, a negative attitude drains your energy and the energy of those with whom you come in contact.

A positive attitude helps to cope more easily with the daily affairs of life. It brings optimism into your life, and makes it easier to avoid worry and negative thinking. If you adopt it as a way of life, it will bring constructive changes into your life, and make you happier, brighter and more successful. With a positive attitude you see the bright side of life, become optimistic and expect the best to happen. It is certainly a state of mind that is well worth developing and strengthening.

Having a positive attitude can help you cope much more easily with life's daily affairs. A positive attitude brings optimism into your life, and makes it easier to avoid worry and negative thinking. If you adopt it as a way of life, it will bring constructive changes into your life and in the long run make you happier and much more successful. It's true. With a positive attitude you will begin to see the bright side of life; you will become optimistic and you will expect the best to happen and it will.

A positive attitude builds courage and fervor into a person. Whether you are hoping to grow a business, overcome a bad boss or just enjoy a better, healthier lifestyle, your attitude significantly impacts your results. The attitude you have will determine the actions you take which will determine the results you get. Your attitude is one of the critical success factors in your life. One exciting thing about that, though, is that you can control your attitude and this book gives you the keys on how to control it so you may win in life and really win big.

How we handle stress depends upon our attitude. Our attitude can also affect the way stress handles us. Optimists are able to cope more effectively with stress. It also reduces their chances of developing stress-related illness.

When optimistic people do become ill, they tend to recover more quickly. Pessimists are likely to deny the problem, distance themselves from the stressful event, focus on stressful feelings, or allow the stressor to interfere with their achievement of a goal. People with a more pessimistic attitude tend to report poorer health compared to people with optimistic attitudes. People with positive attitudes view situations differently from those with negative attitudes. Here are some general statements. Think about how you would respond to them: Positive attitude is:

In times of uncertainty, you should usually expect the best.

In times of uncertainty, you should usually expect the worst.

Look on the bright side of things.

Look on the dark side of things.

Hardly ever expect things to go your way.

Do not always expect things to go your way. When they do not, try to learn something from the experience.

A positive attitude leads to happiness and success and can change your whole life. If you look at the bright side of life, your whole life becomes filled with light. This light affects not only you and the way you look at the world, but also your whole environment and the people around you. If it is strong enough, it becomes contagious. A positive attitude influences our aging. You may not be as young as you feel, but research has found that a positive attitude may delay the ageing process. The University of Texas found that people with an upbeat view of life were less likely than pessimists to show signs of frailty.[3] Again, positive attitude is good for the heart, according to a recent study. The most optimistic among a group of 545 Dutch men aged 64 to 84 had a roughly 50% lower risk of cardiovascular death over 15 years of follow-up, according to the study published in the Archives of Internal Medicine. [4] *"Become a Possibilitarian. No matter how dark things seem to be or actually are, raise your sights and see possibilities—always see them, for they're always there."* - Norman Vincent Peale

Do not take difficult people's behavior personally. In other words, be wise enough not to make personalities out of your hostile environment. Their troublesome behavior is habitual and affects most people with whom they come in contact. Do not fight back or try to beat them at their own games. They have been practicing their skills for a life time, and you are an amateur. Some counselors would advise that you devise a means to deal with difficult colleagues in a payback mode. They say spread rumours too against those who do the same to you. Do not try to appease them. Difficult people have an insatiable appetite for more. Do not try to change them. You can only change your responses to their behavior. This retaliatory model does not meet with divine expectations. Instead, positively model your attitude to be the exact opposite of their harassment.

Change your attitude towards the difficult person, and remain positive in your approach. Usually, the difficult person is someone who is working from the negative side of their personality, rather than someone with a conscious passion to be difficult. The difficult person is sometimes unaware of themselves and how their negative attitude affects others, though some are well aware and do enjoy the game. But, we must point out that some of these difficult colleagues are unaware how harmful their actions are to their own career success. In the business world, we are constantly faced with trying to work with others who may challenge our ability to get things done. There is great value to be gained when we take the time to try to understand another's viewpoint. By changing our attitude toward them and changing our viewpoint about what makes them "wrong", we can find a wealth of knowledge to improve our own ability to work with people.

Replace negative, inappropriate reactions with different, more acceptable ones. Even though it is the job of a negativist to change his or her actions, you may need to know that some of these persons may not know what to do differently in order to come across as more positive. It will often be up to you to specify exactly what that is. You can deliberately decide to begin to search out the person's great qualities or contributions now being eclipsed by the negative behavior. You can prevent their negativity by instilling in them the positivist bug. If you do that, they may never catch the negativity virus again. Be the role model for speech, conduct, behaviour, reaction to pain etc.

Keeping a positive mental outlook is for certain the most important aspect of survival. While in a survival situation you need to practice self-reliance. You will only be able to depend on yourself and your abilities. You will have to overcome many challenges that you are not accustomed to. Modern society is conditioned to instant relief from discomforts such as darkness, hunger, pain, thirst, boredom, cold, and heat. Adapt yourself and tolerate any that you face. It is only temporary. When you first realize that you are in a hostile environment, stop and regain your composure. Control your anger; recognize dangers to your career, learn to relax and think; do not make any hasty judgments about the persons involved or the situation at hand. Be sure to keep cool, calm, coordinated and collected. It is important to make the right approach at all times using your best ability.

Never give up on your dream and career. Prepare for the worst in the place where you are, but hope for the best. This is because, in the corporate world, where you are is only a learning ground for where you will be. Thus, you better learn the lessons now, so that you will be a master tomorrow.

Also, make positive affirmations a lifestyle. Positive affirmations are faith builders. Affirmations are positive sentences that describe a desired situation, and which are repeated many times, in order to impress the subconscious mind and trigger it into positive action. In order to ensure the effectiveness of the affirmations, they have to be repeated with attention, conviction, interest and desire.

The only one who can put limits on God is you! If you can find a scripture to stand on, a promise to hold on to, God will never fail you. The only variable is you. Are you going to search out the scriptures? Are you going to find God's promises for you? Are you going to believe God no matter what the circumstances may say? If not, you going to be ruled by every wind and wave that passes your way. Are you going to let the circumstances of life dictate your future? Refuse to do that; you serve the great I AM, El Shaddai, Jehovah Jireh. There is absolutely no reason on earth for you to be ruled by life's circumstances. Choose to see God in all of His power and glory, and by doing that, problems, no matter how small or great, are nothing in comparison to Him.

Shape your perspective and monitor your self-talk. Are you aware of the inner dialogue you carry on with yourself during your waking hours? Do you say critical and negative things to yourself such as "I am always making errors," or "That is just my luck," or "I am no good at office relationships?" The more frequently these negative thoughts are repeated, the stronger they become. The first step in overcoming negative self-talk is to become aware of it. The next step is to replace these self-defeating thoughts with positive and productive ones. Listen to the internal dialogue going on inside you. Divide one or more sheets of paper into two columns and, for a few days, jot down in the left column all the negative thoughts that come into your head. Rewrite each thought in a positive way in the second column. Practise doing this in your mind until it becomes a habit.

Change your vocabulary. In his latest bestseller, Anthony Robbins tells how he was able to lower the intensity of his anger by changing the words he used to describe his emotional state. Instead of saying he was "angry and upset," he chose to say, "I feel myself getting a 'bit peeved'." Robbins believes that our choice of words can not only lower the intensity of our negative emotions, but it can also intensify our positive emotions. For example, when someone asks how you are doing, instead of saying "all right," say "superb." Robbins suggests, "Notice the words you habitually use and replace them with ones that empower you."[5]

More than often people repeat negative sentences and statements, concerning diverse situations in their lives, and consequently bring upon themselves undesirable situations. Affirmations work both ways, to build and to destroy. They are a kind of a neutral power. It is the way we use them that determines whether they are going to bring good or harmful results. Affirmations are similar to creative visualization. The repeated words build mental images and scenes in the mind. The words help to focus on the aim, object or situation one wants to achieve or create. Frequent repetitions make the subconscious mind accept them, and then it influences and affects the way one thinks, acts and behaves.

Affirmations work like commands that are given to a computer. They influence us, other people, events and circumstances. It might seem strange to you, but they do also influence the people we meet, our circumstances and the events we encounter. Sometimes they work fast, but more often they need time. Repeating positive affirmations a few minutes, and then thinking negatively, neutralizes the effects of the positive words. You have to refuse negative thoughts; otherwise you will not attain positive results.

We often repeat affirmations, without even being aware of the process. We use them when we tell ourselves that we can't do something, that we are too lazy, or when we believe we are going to fail. The subconscious mind always accepts and follows what we tell it. It is the same principle at work when we say to ourselves that we can do it, or we cannot, when we say we are going to succeed or when we keep saying that we are going to fail. It is the same power working both ways. Why not choose the better way? Attitudes can even be detected in the words we use. For example, "I would not," indicates choice, whereas "I cannot" indicates powerlessness.

There should be no physical, emotional or mental tension while repeating them. The stronger the concentration, the more faith you have in what you are doing; the more feelings you put into the act, the stronger and faster will be the results. It is very important to choose only positive affirmations. For example you desire to delight in your job in spite of the torments, do not say, "I am sad, I am going to be happy." By saying this sentence you are repeating to your subconscious mind that you are not happy. The word "sad" also evokes negative images. It is better to say, "My job has an attached happiness, and I have the right to be healthy in it". Such words evoke positive images in the mind.

It is important to affirm in the present tense, not the future tense. Saying: "I will survive this", means that you intend to be an overcomer one day, in the indefinite future. You are actually telling yourself that some day you will be rich, never now. It is better and more effective to say, and also feel, "I am an overcomer; "I am overcoming now", and the subconscious mind will work overtime to make this happen now, in the present. As to results, sometimes they may come fast, and at other times may take more time to manifest. Achieving results through the power of affirmations depends on how much time, energy, faith and feelings you invest in your affirmations, on how big or small is your goal, and on how strong is your desire.

By using the power of affirmations you state what you want to be true in your life. You see reality, as you want it to be in your hostile environment. For a while, you ignore your current circumstances and your difficulties, and concentrate on a different reality. God is willing to cross it with you. He is committed to communicating with His people and to providing strength, comfort, and hope. If you are up against a wall and want to know how to deal with it, do not try to overcome under your own strength.

Learn to understand your own personality and your unique strengths and weaknesses. Most of us do not know ourselves at all. It is then explainable why we easily fail under pressure. In a hostile environment you will be pushed to the wall, positioned to make deliberate errors, commit administrative blunders and even moral flaws. Most of these career threatening factors are planned and well strategized by your harassers, but how you put your ability to work with wisdom will determine your survival. Ability has to do with how well you manage your emotions, take the knocks, approach issues and still come out standing. Therefore, put your ability to test because you have what it takes to live and survive in any situation. We have an in-built mechanism to turn our situations around if we so desire. The hostile situation can become fun for you if you so desire. Learn to recognize when your defensive mechanisms come up. Realize that you are probably not really being attacked. When you catch yourself feeling defensive, do not react so quickly. Learn how to listen when someone asks a question or makes a suggestion without reading too many meanings into the words. The effort to improve your ability to get along with others will be rewarded as you find more career opportunities open up for you.

Survival depends a great deal on a person's ability to withstand stress in hostile environments. Your brain is without doubt your best survival tool. It is your most valuable asset in a survival situation. It is not always the physically strong who are the most effective or better at handling hostile colleagues or situations. Survival more often depends on your reactions to the harsh situation created by difficult co-workers. To survive learn how to adapt to your situation; adaptation is the key to life. A person's psychological reaction to a hostile environment depends on his or her ability to use his or her shock absorbers. With the proper attitude almost anything is possible. To make it through the worst, a strong will or determination to live is needed. A powerful desire to continue living is a must. The mind has the power to will the body to extraordinary feats.

Without the will to live, survival is impossible. Survival is possible in most situations, but it demands a lot of will-power. A commitment to live, refusal to give up, and positive mental attitude greatly increases your chances of survival. Do not add any extra burden to yourself by falling into a destructive mental state like feeling self-pity or hopelessness. Remember the important aspects of your life and do not let the image fade. Consider every loss as an opportunity to explore new areas. With the proper attitude your experience could be interesting. Enjoy the challenge. Or else, If you have to work with difficult people every day, you probably dread going to work each morning. What is more, you might get so stressed that you cannot concentrate on the job, but rely on your will power and build up your inner strength.

Manage your anger with wisdom. People who are easily angered generally have what some psychologists call a low or zero tolerance level for frustration. At this level, some persons feel that they should not be subjected to frustration, disgrace, pain, anguish, insult, slight, inconvenience, or annoyance. These types of people lack the ability to take things in stride, and they are always infuriated if the situation seems unjust or unfair, that is when justice is denied them. Since we all have a propensity to anger, how we manage it is a serious part of our survival in the hostile environment.

According to Charles Spielberger, anger is "an emotional state that varies in intensity from mild irritation to intense fury and rage."[6] Like other emotions, anger is accompanied by physiological and biological changes in the human body. When you get angry, your heart rate and blood pressure go up. Similarly, the levels of your energy hormones rise, as does both adrenaline, and noradrenalin levels.[7] Due to these changes, there is a rise in a voice level or tone, colour of our eyes, and inflection. However, anger is a completely normal, healthy, human emotion. It is only when it gets out of control that it turns destructive, leads to problems at work, personal relationships, and in the overall quality of human life.

Anger can be caused by both external and internal events. You could be angry at a specific person such as a co-worker or supervisor, event such as promotion, annual staff party and awards, or by worrying or brooding about your difficult colleagues or superiors at work. Sometimes due to the ill feelings we have in our work, living or learning environments, memories of traumatic or enraging events can also trigger angry feelings in us.

The instinctive, natural way to express anger is to respond to the situation or person aggressively. Anger is a natural, adaptive response to threats; it inspires powerful, often aggressive, feelings and behaviors, which allow us to fight and to defend ourselves when we are attacked. A certain amount of anger, therefore, is necessary for our survival. But, do not be unmindful of the fact that your harasser or difficult colleagues expect you to react angrily. When you do, you have fallen into the game plan to either eliminate you or frustrate you more. Therefore, learn to be calm, do not lash out at every person or object that irritates or annoys us. In fact, laws, social norms, and common sense place limits on how far our anger can take us. Ephesians 4:26 says "Be angry, and sin not: do not allow the sun go down upon your wrath."

People use a variety of both conscious and unconscious processes to deal with their angry feelings. The three main approaches are expressing, suppressing, and calming. Expressing your angry feelings in an assertive— not aggressive—manner is the healthiest way to express anger. To do this, you have to learn how to make clear what your needs are, and how to get them met, without hurting others. By this you are being respectful of yourself and others.

Anger can be suppressed, and then converted or redirected. This happens when you hold in your anger, stop thinking about it, and focus on something positive. The aim is to inhibit or suppress your anger and convert it into more constructive behavior. The danger in this type of response is that if it is not allowed outward expression, your anger can turn inward—on yourself. Anger turned inward may cause high blood pressure, or depression. People who are constantly putting others down, criticizing everything and making cynical comments are usually manifesting inward anger. You can also calm down inside, asking the Holy Spirit to take control. Slowly repeat a spiritual word or prayer to yourself such as "father, take control." This means not just controlling or expressing a spiritual wish to control your outward behavior, but also a passion to have dominion over your inner push and feelings. As you do these, use an image to visualize a relaxing experience, from either your memory or your imagination to help you calm your mind or emotion.

Simply put, this means changing the way you think. Angry people tend to curse, swear, or speak in highly colourful terms that reflect their inner thoughts. When you are angry, your thinking can get much exaggerated and overly dramatic. Try replacing these thoughts with more rational ones. For instance, instead of telling yourself, "Oh, it is nasty, it is terrible, everything is ruined," tell yourself, "it is frustrating, and it is understandable that I am upset about it, but it is not the end of the world and getting angry is not going to fix it anyhow." Be careful of words like "never" or "always" when talking about yourself or someone else. They will alienate and humiliate people who might otherwise not be willing to work with you.

Anger does not fix a problem, rather it worsens it. Remind yourself that getting angry is not going to fix anything that it would not make you feel better (and may actually make you feel worse). Logic defeats anger, because anger, even when it is justified, can quickly become irrational. So use cold hard logic on yourself. Remind yourself that the world is "not out to get you," you are just experiencing some of the rough spots of daily life. Do this each time you feel anger getting the best of you, and it will help you get a more balanced perspective.

Avoid hostilities when you are angry. Angry people tend to jump to and act on conclusions and some of those conclusions can be very inaccurate. These are incidentally the errors your harassers want you to fall into. When you are confronted and cornered in a hostile work, living or learning environment and anger works up on you, slow down and think through your responses. Do not say the first thing that comes into your head, but slow down and think carefully about what you want to say. At the same time, listen carefully to what the other person is saying and take your time before answering.

To manage your anger, listen to your heart to find out the cause of your anger. Listen, too, to what is underlying the anger. For instance, you might like a certain amount of freedom and personal initiative, and your "significant other" wants more connection and control. If he or she starts complaining about your activities, do not retaliate by painting your partner as a jailer, a warden, or an albatross around your neck. It is natural to get defensive when you are criticized, but do not fight back. Instead, listen to what is underlying the words: the message that this person might feel neglected and unloved. It may take a lot of patient questioning on your part, and it may require some breathing space, but do not let your anger or a partner's let a discussion spin out of control. Keeping your cool can keep the situation from becoming a disastrous one.

Manage your anger by giving yourself a break. Sometimes it is our immediate surroundings that give us cause for irritation and fury. Problems and responsibilities can weigh on you and make you feel angry at the "trap" you seem to have fallen into and all the people and things that form that trap. Give yourself a break. The things that causes you anger might be because you avoid positive office politics. Office politics is not harmful. Those who refuse to play it suffer the most. Think and think well!

CHAPTER FIVE:

DO NOT AVOID POSITIVE OFFICE POLITICS.

1 ¶ Now Saul spoke to Jonathan his son and to all his servants, that they should kill David;2 but Jonathan, Saul's son, delighted greatly in David. So Jonathan told David, saying, "My father Saul seeks to kill you. Therefore please be on your guard until morning, and stay in a secret place and hide.3 "And I will go out and stand beside my father in the field where you are, and I will speak with my father about you. Then what I observe, I will tell you."4 Thus Jonathan spoke well of David to Saul his father, and said to him, "Let not the king sin against his servant, against David, because he has not sinned against you, and because his works have been very good toward you.5 "For he took his life in his hands and killed the Philistine, and the LORD brought about a great deliverance for all Israel. You saw it and rejoiced. Why then will you sin against innocent blood, to kill David without a cause?"6 So Saul heeded the voice of Jonathan, and Saul swore, "As the LORD lives, he shall not be killed."7 Then Jonathan called David, and Jonathan told him all these things. So Jonathan brought David to Saul, and he was in his presence as in times past.8 ¶ And there was war again; and David went out and fought with the Philistines, and struck them with a mighty blow, and they fled from him.9 Now the distressing spirit from the LORD came upon Saul as he sat in his house with his spear in his hand. And David was playing music with his hand. And Saul sought to pin David to the wall with the spear, but he slipped away from Saul's presence; and he drove the spear into the wall. So David fled and escaped that night. (1 Samuel 19: 1 – 10 NKJV).

Some of us believe that in any place where one find oneself whether at work, school or business, the only way to get the best, do well and advance and shine on the job, all one needs, is hard work, a good character, an excellent work ethic, talent, and a determination to succeed. According to DuBrin, if you hold such beliefs, you are best classified as an "Innocent Lamb" in the modern world of office and business success politics.[1]

All workplaces today, even living and learning environments, are affected by the intrigues of politics. These intrigues are what we refer to as "office politics." Some of us are working, living or learning in a hostile environment because we have not looked deeply into the political terrain in which we do business. Some of us would usually even boost about it that we do not have time for office politics. Beloved, in the corporate business world, the only persons who suffer from office politics are those who refuse to play it.

According to Aristotle "Man is by nature political."[2] So, no organization, home, school or institution is politics-free, but there are organizations where politics plays a minor role. If things at your company seem truly irremediable, it might be time to start looking deeply. You do not have to work in an office to be familiar with office politics. Anyone who has ever had any job, anywhere, knows that the dynamics among those who are part of the work environment play an important part in how a business is run. Sometimes, when we talk of office politics, what comes to people's mind is "forming secret alliances and exchanging favors"—these are all negative aspects of office politics that come to mind for most people. DuBrin,[3] however, asserts that playing office politics is important for maintaining and advancing one's career and for self-protection to which I agree in toto.

Office politics is something most people recognize when they see it in action, but find difficult to define. Office Politics involves "...the use and misuse of power in the workplace."[4] Office politics is nothing more than developing and maintaining effective working relationships with people relevant to your company or business. This can include employees, customers, consultants and contractors, anyone who has influence on your job, company and industry. "Playing politics" therefore is nothing more than maintaining good working relationships. Apparently office politics is an increasing problem. According to a study by Accountemps, "Eighteen percent of an administrator's time more than nine weeks out of every year -- is spent resolving conflicts among employees"[5]

In the article "Seven Career Killers," Erin Burt warns "avoiding politics altogether can be deadly for your career. Every workplace has an intricate system of power, and you can, and should work it ethically to your best advantage."[6] By becoming politically adept you can learn to rise above power plays and interpersonal conflicts, build a reputation as a go-to person, expert, or leader, or gain access to resources, information and opportunities and Influence outcomes and get buy-in for ideas and initiatives.

Play the politics of relationship. In David's court job, we find serious work politics at play. Saul the boss was already fed up with David and wanted him killed. He mentioned it to all his servants or rather workers, David must be removed out of the way. However, in the midst of this turbulence and hostile environment, David had someone in the corridor of power that could save his career and life from political death. Jonathan, the Son of Saul delighted in David. The term "delighted" (châphêts) means be pleased, favoured and desirable. Only Jonathan could reveal the Father's evil plot to David. It was because David knew how to play the politics of the palace. To survive, do not avoid positive office politics.

From the life and attitude of David, there is a message for people who say they cannot stomach office politics: You will die a slow, painful career death. This is because there is no getting around office politics, and mastering them is essential to being able to steer your own career. Office politics is inescapable because it's about dealing with the people. When there is a group of people anywhere, even on the playground, there is politics. Survival in a hostile environment demands that you do not avoid positive office politics.

When you are in a place, learn to identify the people and places where power resides. Some of these might be official, while others are not. By this, I mean that there are people who, due to their position in a company, actually are power brokers, but there are some others who do not occupy a position but do in reality hold power. So, identify people with whom to build relationships, and these should be your superiors. These relationships are those that will help you to succeed when the chips are down.

Form strategic alliances by making yourself valuable to those with power, knowledge or tenure. In prison as well as in the office, there are those with official power and unofficial power. Someone in a position of authority can, in reality, turn out to be very weak. For example, a prison guard who does not get along well with his or her boss and who is seen as overly friendly to the inmates holds power. Conversely, someone in a low official capacity can turn out to have a lot of power and influence. For example, the confidential secretary to the president of the company who controls their calendar and schedule of meetings and who holds their trust does in actuality hold power.

Go out of your way to offer power brokers assistance. Some superiors actually need help to move up in the corporate ladder. Give them help where you can no matter how inconvenient it is for you today. Remember, one good turn deserves another. When you need help, you'll have established a network of supporters. When your superior has a project such as you have the expertise in, offer your help, it may not be appreciated, but the role you have played cannot be forgotten. Perform deliberate acts of kindness. Stay late one night to help a co-worker on a deadline. Send a handwritten thank-you note to the person who gave you that Word tip. One of my daughters who is a banker worked with a particularly difficult boss: a lady. What she did not know was that her lady boss was having a terrible marital crisis: she lacked affirmation, acceptance and appreciation in her home which made her to take out her frustration on her subordinates. My daughter and her colleagues began to affirm their boss's beauty, commend her hair style, make up and clothes. Sometimes they went as far as asking "madam" to take them to her saloon to fix their hair. As this affirmation and commendation went on relationship improved and job became less stressful and hostile. What they did was to offer emotional assistance to a superior who needed it to also survive. Little things matters!

In relationship politics, pay your dues where you have to. In fact Jesus said "give to Caesar what belongs to Caesar and to God what belongs to God."[7] Pay your dues by a culture of greeting. If your boss is the one who loves to be greeted, when you come to the office, go ahead and do so if it makes him/her feel important, in control and significant, go ahead. After all, it does not take away anything from you. Rather it speaks volume of your character. Keep building a track record for paying your dues all over again, while networking with people who are in favor so that your new reputation blossoms and can be later harvested. Some of these dues we are to pay have to do with social outings, and events or occasions of note in the life of our superiors or colleagues. Where there is a party, an obituary ceremony where all workers would be present, a company dinner and other such events, why stay out. Most times our point for keeping away from such ceremonies is because of the "ungodly" atmosphere of music, dance and alcohol among others. But, remember that attending does not warrant you to partake in ungodly excesses. Nobody has said you must do the ungodly thing there, but do you forbid people even when they are wrong in attitude? So, you can make a difference.

In office life your supervisor holds the power of life and death over you (at least as it concerns your career). The most important aspect of working in an office is getting along with your boss and others in power and managing your relationship with them. Because the happier they are, the happier and more comfortable you will be. In prison, the ones who get the beat down and who get thrown to the wolves are the problem inmates: the ones who cause problems and troubles for those in power. Note that the definition of people in power is not necessarily just the warden or prison guards, but fellow inmates. Be careful in a hostile environment, negotiate well the power relationships in the office and your life will be much easier.

Where there is party organized by the boss, show up. Even if the party is a total bore, stay for at least an hour or an hour and a half. Before you leave, show your face to the celebrant, thank the person who organized the party and the one who approved or financed the expenditure. When bosses are trying to decide, if they can trust you with clients and promotion, your manners like this count. If the occasion is by invitation, if invited, this is a fine time do prepare your spouse. Your spouse should know the names of your close co-workers and senior managers. If there is company gossip you have let slip at home and should not have, made sure your spouse stays mum.

When it is especially a company social event, do attend. Your office holiday party, cocktail evening, etcetera is not an optional event. "Even if you hate these things, it is a good idea to put in an appearance, because it shows you are part of the team." says Marjorie Brody.[8] Therefore, dress professionally; treat the ceremony as Work, Not Play. Remember, it is a business occasion. Would you go to a business event and get drunk or spend the whole night talking to your buddies? If not, don't do it here. While you are there, use the time to socialize with co-workers you don't normally see and, of course, the boss. But don't just talk business. Do not be the office bore. Get to know people. Be festive. Have fun. Observe people. If someone is wearing a broach or pendant with a inscription or symbol, it's pretty much permission to talk about the rainbow. Find something, and there is always something around someone with which to break the ice in interaction.

Play the politics of respect. In our text, David respected Saul in spite of the harm he wanted to do to him. When Jonathan chose to speak to his father about the problem on ground, David still showed respect both to Saul and to Jonathan. The age difference between David and Jonathan was very little, yet that did not stop David from paying due obeisance to Jonathan as the kings Son. Similarly, David recognized Jonathan's position to speak and act on the matter. David did not show disrespect to Jonathan by abusing him over his father's action. He was not insolent or saucy in speech, he kept his respect for the power structure and it led to his survival. Respect makes you likeable.

Respect people's position and work.[9] In so doing, refer to them by title or by position. There are superiors and even colleagues who love to be addressed by their titles: Dr, architect, engineer, pharmacist, etc.

Be wise enough to place this into your vocabulary in your business transactions and official relationships. Every human organization is both an official and unofficial, formal and informal network of relationships and coalitions. Therefore, learn to study your shadow organization and you will understand how power and influence play out. Investigate your shadow organization by playing the role of an observer, as though you are a corporate anthropologist. Notice who has influence, and who gets along with whom. Discover who is respected and who champions others. Who are the hubs of social interaction and corporate intelligence? Find out who really gets things done. [10]

Recognize the role and work of each person and appreciate them. The act of making yourself likeable is office politicking. You should not fake it if you are a genuinely nice and interested person. If office politics requires you to do something fake, consider it that you were not likeable in the first place. For you, office politics is a training ground to teach yourself to be likeable, and, as a side benefit, you will save your job. For others, office politics is the time at work when you get to be your best, true, self in search of more learning opportunities and more human connections.[11]

Follow the chain of command in carrying out your official assignments. Do not bye-pass your superior no matter how genuine your intentions are. You would have slighted both your superior's person and position. You see, damage control is a very difficult thing to do in a work environment. Managers who do not follow the chain of command are termed rebels. The structure is in place to manage the overwhelming load of information and decision making in the organization. If a supervisor or manager does an "end run" around his or her boss and brings an issue to the executive, without using the existing channels, is likely to be sent back down the ladder to resolve it where it belongs.[12]

A friend was in haste to do an outstanding job and be ready for what was to come; overlooked coordination with the data center manager, and the director. Thus, being people and fallible, and probably slightly insecure, they thought he had "evil" intent. That is, they thought he wanted to make himself look good at their expense in the eyes of senior management, and therefore enhance his promotion possibilities. Knowing my friend as I do, I knew nothing could be further from the truth. He wanted to make his "boss" look good. But by the time he had figured out the mistake, it was (as is usual in these matters) irreparable.

Do we have respect for those in low places, especially if they are an older folk than us? When we learn to respect the lowly placed for their age and not for their position because they do not have one, you shall have a safe haven of work. Cultivating the leaders of your organization will create opportunities for you. But to do your job you will have to also cultivate secretaries, janitors and all those people who govern how things really get done in organizations. Respect helps you get along well with others. Executives do not want to do damage control or get dragged into resolving differences. If you cannot work and play well with others, you will not last long. Cross any of these people and you will suffer consequences either officially as in the results of your performance review, or unofficially, in how much or how little access you will have to the boss or how cooperative the various departments will be with you in getting your projects done.

In playing the politics of respect sometimes ask your respected higher-ups for counsel about your official assignments. Encourage them to think of you as a protégé, and they are more likely to defend you when you need it. Most executives have earned their rank the hard way—learning the business, working in the trenches, navigating the politics. So a newcomer who underestimates them or discounts their experience is going to get their punishment.[13]

Play the politics of responsibility. In the text David continued with his official job with fervour and dedication. He knew there was danger at work, yet he put his mind to work as always. In fact, it was known by all that David was a symbol of victory. This is a mark of responsibility. Some of us are in hostile environments because we are not responsible with work. In business, who you know can become more important than what you know Keep developing relationships with key power holders who will help you influence the "King" subtly and informally by hopefully dropping your name and working your efforts into their conversation. Since you know you turned off the King by advocating for a cause that was not near and dear to him, figure out those initiatives that are his babies and, if they are consistent with your value system, work on supporting them. Do not be too obvious about these new efforts, since diligent, conscientious work behind the scenes will impress him even more than flamboyant, spotlight grabbing ones. Each day in business, a corporate version of "survival of the fittest" is played out. Power plays, turf battles, deception, and sabotage block individuals' career progress and threaten companies' resources and results. A good place to start is pitfalls to avoid.[14]

No Overly-detailed presentation is a mark of responsibility. Most executives do not want the details or the chronological front-to-back history of an issue. They want to get to the heart of the matter and hear the answers to questions such as, "What is the problem?" "What do you recommend?" "Why do you think that is the best solution?" "How much will it cost?" Hold your details in reserve, in case you are asked for more information. Be prepared to cut your presentation in half, if the agenda gets squeezed at the last minute.

No official job surprise for the boss is a mark of responsibility. Managers, who do not share bad news with their boss or give fair warning when a problem is brewing, will soon learn the error of their ways. Executives are expected to be well-briefed about the details of their operation. It is always better to err on the side of honest disclosure with a battle plan about how to fix the problem.

Do whatever it takes to get the job done.[15] Most executives do not have much tolerance for directors who do not do "whatever it takes" to get the job done. Even if you have to be home to pick up the kids from day care, you need to take work home or work on Saturday, if that is what is required.

Do the job for now and not lobby for promotion. Most executives distrust managers who have their eyes on their next promotion rather than on the job at hand. They also take a dim view of a manager who is obviously jockeying for a bigger position, or for more power. All things being equal, they are more likely to promote the person whose first priority is the organization, rather than themselves.

Manage risks to your level of ability. Executives expect the leaders to lead. When a manager lacks the courage to confront problems or people, it usually turns into a cancer that grows and multiplies. By the time it is a crisis, the executive is involved—and not happy about it. Shun Complacency. Smart executives recognize that if the business is not growing and changing, it is dying. And if the executive's team loses that scrappy, competitive edge and sense of urgency, the business is already sick. Arrogance is a dangerous thing.

Whenever the subject of politics comes up, we all tend to focus on backstabbing and brown-nosing. We forget that there are also "positive" politics-building communities, looking out for people, avoiding the temptation to do self-serving things. Do a favour for someone and you will find that you add to your political capital and create a more positive place to work. If you want to be at the top, you cannot stand above politics. There is not any above or outside. There is politics, warfare or oblivion. You can sometimes change the rules of the game but not the game itself. Make your choice.[16] One way you change the rules of the game of politics and how you play it, is to find yourself a mentor. A mentor is the hand that guides and leads you through both known and unknown paths of life to make the best out of the opportunities and challenges in the hostile environment.

CHAPTER SIX:

FIND YOURSELF A MENTOR.

So David fled and escaped, and went to Samuel at Ramah, and told him all that Saul had done to him. And he and Samuel went and stayed in Naioth. Now it was told Saul, saying, "Take note, David is at Naioth in Ramah!" Then Saul sent messengers to take David. And when they saw the group of prophets prophesying, and Samuel standing as leader over them, the Spirit of God came upon the messengers of Saul, and they also prophesied. And when Saul was told, he sent other messengers, and they prophesied likewise. Then Saul sent messengers again the third time, and they prophesied also. Then he also went to Ramah, and came to the great well that is at Sechu. So he asked, and said, "Where are Samuel and David?" And someone said, "Indeed they are at Naioth in Ramah."23 So he went there to Naioth in Ramah. Then the Spirit of God was upon him also, and he went on and prophesied until he came to Naioth in Ramah. And he also stripped off his clothes and prophesied before Samuel in like manner, and lay down naked all that day and all that night. Therefore they say, "Is Saul also among the prophets?" (1 Samuel 19: 18 – 24 NKJV).

The Ukwuani people say that "you do not call a single person society." The import of this statement is that a tree does not make a forest. Everyone who is hoping for a boost in his or job growth or working life needs someone else to fall on and depend on. The living, learning and work environment is sometimes nasty, naughty and terrible. There is where you need a level of outside help and support to survive. *"Behind every successful person, there is one elementary truth: somewhere, somehow, someone cared about their growth and development. This person was their Mentor."* [1] A mentor then is a factor for success.

The Merriam-Webster online Dictionary defines a mentor as "a trusted counselor or guide."[2] Similarly, a mentor is "a wise, loyal advisor."[3] A mentor is an individual, usually older, always more experienced, who helps and guides another individual's development. A mentor is that one person who can guide you, help you, take you under his or her wing, and nurture your career quest.

The term 'mentor' has a long history, going back to Homer's famous poem the *Odyssey*. When King Odysseus left to fight in the Trojan War, his friend Mentor, an Ithacan nobleman, was trusted with the care of his son, Telemachus. During Odysseus' ten year absence Mentor was a stand-in for Odysseus, and had to "personify the kingly quality of wisdom." Telemachus was having a difficult time fending off suitors from his mother, Penelope, since everyone assumed that Odysseus was dead and would not return from his voyages. Although it all works out in the end, Penelope's wait certainly would have been more troubled without the guiding hand of the mentor.[4]

Although not a biblical word, mentoring appears to be a biblical concept, as Mallison contends "Mentoring was a way of life in Bible times."[5] Lawrie explains that, there are stories of followers of God who took younger followers under their wing, providing counsel, challenging beliefs, demonstrating a lifestyle of faith. As each generation faced the challenges of discovering what it meant to be God's people, they benefited from the wisdom and experience of those who came before them.[6] In the Bible, there are numerous examples of mentoring, such as the relationship of Barnabas to Paul, Paul to Titus, Elizabeth to Mary, Naomi to Ruth, Moses and Joshua, as well as David with Samuel.

A mentor is a person who has a positive and enduring impact on your personal or professional life. **Find yourself a mentor -- or let a mentor find you.** A mentor is that one person who has long-term commitment and a deep-seated investment in your future. The aim of seeking a mentor is to increase your individual competence to handle situations, activate your personal ability to operate at various levels in your stress-filled business and enhance your personal capacity to deliver. As young professionals, career women, young academics, students, house wives or whatever, you need a mentor to survive in a hostile environment.[7]

David sought out Samuel when things began to go rough and tough. He remembered the Prophet who sought him out from nowhere, the prophet who believed in his abilities, and the prophet who conferred royal and divine authority on him. David felt that it was necessary to run into him in times of crisis. But, as with everything in life, we need to make good decisions and choices in selecting the people we want to emulate. A good mentor can make a world of difference in how we succeed and progress in our careers. Keep in mind that mentors can serve a variety of purposes.

A mentor is someone you can talk with without fear of a backlash, a person whom you can cry before and open up all your fears and pains to without feeling ashamed or inferior. A mentor is someone who by way of position or age has wisdom that is only acquired through experience. Keep an open mind, you cannot survive alone. Find a mentor or let one find you.

He or she would be able to help you in ways you had not planned for or did not expect. Your circle of friends and family represent a good starting point in the search for mentors. From there, expand your search to include teachers, leaders of groups to which you belong, spiritual or religious leaders, and other significant people in your life. Research shows that mentoring relationships can be instrumental in career success.[8] Mentors provide advice and guidance, help instill confidence and offer reassurance, as well as link their "mentee" to a network of contacts that will be useful throughout their career. It is important to choose a mentor whose goals are similar to your own. A mentor's status is irrelevant; it is the interpersonal qualities that count.[9]

Find a mentor who is spiritual.[10] Mentoring is a one-to-one relationship that focuses on the needs of the mentored participant. It encourages that individual to develop to their fullest potential - spiritually and emotionally. Regardless of age, mature Christian men, women, pastors and deacons can be godly role models in our search for excellence and survival in our hostile environment. David did the best thing in life that should be done during a time of crisis, he ran into his mentor who was a prophet and a priest. When Saul was informed that David was with Samuel at Naioth, he sent his servants to pick him, but Samuel was ministering at that time with David in the place and the spirit of God came down mightily. What a mentor to have.

What happens physically have a spiritual origin; therefore it becomes necessary to have a mentor who understands the workings of the spiritual realm. Your mentor is one who can prophesy over your life and invoke the power of the Spirit upon you. He ministers to your fear, cancels the fears, speaks faith into your spirit man and builds a spiritual shield around you as Samuel did for David. Among the company of prophets under Samuel prophesying, was David, though not prophesying but being ministered to. Samuel was standing and presiding over the ministration. The term "standing" (amad) means to stand behind someone or something, to repair, ordain, confirm, fasten, or make to be still.[11] Similarly, the term "preside" (nâtsab) means to settle, sharpen and establish.[12] Thus, Samuel was repairing David's broken spirit and affirming him at the same time.

So what we find taking place was not an ordinary prophetic outburst, it was a deliberate ministration for a David in dire need of succour and sustenance. A spiritual mentor uses his or her spiritual gifts and spirituality to help and influence others. Spiritual mentors have skills to interpret dreams, determine your life's purpose, and assist you to use spiritual methods and tools for your business health and overall well being. A Spiritual mentor gives you heightened awareness of the spiritual cloud and atmosphere operating in your hostile environment and helps your mind gain clarity and inner peace through prophetic ministrations to your life.

A spiritual mentor is your prophetic and personal support, one who signifies for you a cheerleader of positive emotions. The spiritual mentor has the word of faith on his or her lips. As Isaiah would say, the spiritual mentor has the tongue of the learned, words seasoned with salt, full of grace and truth. A spiritual mentor can help you to find solace, hope and enhance daily growth in confronting and overcoming your challenge of neglect, verbal assault, physical attacks, official snipping and insults. Spiritual mentors repair your broken spirit, bind up your broken hearts, infuse fresh strength and power into you, build courage in your inner man and give you a sense of divine presence. Spiritual mentors use appropriate spiritual principles and power to sharpen and enhance your skills. Remember, whatever we bind on earth shall have been bound in heaven and whatever we loose on earth shall have been loosed in heaven (Matt. 18:18). A spiritual mentor is your binding and loosing officer.

You need a mentor who is spiritual because there are times when you cannot pray the way you should, moments when you loose a sense of spiritual clarity and pulse. There are moments when trouble, stress and the urge for survival become so great that you need an experienced person to see the things that you cannot see inorder to move on in life. That is why even when you feel you are finished, you want to resign and seek another job, a mentor says no, you still have a destiny where you are.

A Spiritual mentor is important to show that God intrudes in our lives anywhere and anytime. God does not meet us at church, He interacts with us anywhere and every where, even in the daily routines of life. God's Spirit can fill our hearts chauffeuring the kids or feeding the dog. Spiritual mentors are people we listen to, watch and imitate in our daily living. It helps to see how a seasoned believer handles an office crisis or family dispute. If we can open ourselves to such people, the Spirit will take care of the rest. Spiritual mentor's makes faith to be *caught* more than *taught*. A spiritual mentor is someone who opens up the world of faith to you. This was what Samuel did for David. There might be trouble all around you, but you have shelter in the storm with a spiritual mentor under the great shepherd of the sheep.

The spiritual mentor has the gifts and skills of discernment, a listening heart, a gentle and patient spirit, a good working knowledge of the sacred texts and a basic understanding of psychology and counseling. The spiritual mentor provides the opportunity to be more intentional, focused, gives permission to question and grow, and provides assurance of God's unfailing love and enables you to participate more fully in the sacred movement and purpose of life.

Find a mentor who is supportive. A study was undertaken on the Hawaiian island of Kauai by two researchers named Emily Werner and Ruth Smith. This study, which followed more than 450 people from childhood through their adult lives, was an attempt to learn why some people are motivated to overcome severe disadvantages, while others from the same background seem to have been overwhelmed by their problems. This research continued for an incredible length of time: 40 years, to be exact. According to the research, one of the most interesting qualities of these motivated individuals is their ability to recognize potential sources of support in other people, to look beyond the walls of their homes to find relatives, friends, teachers, or other role models who can provide help. This very important finding illustrates the benefits of forming mentor relationships to encourage achievement.[13]

David fled to Samuel and stayed in Naioth. Samuel knew that David was a wanted man in Israel, an enemy of the king and a state security risk, yet he stuck to David. It was a dangerous thing to do because he could be accused and charged with conspiracy for keeping David. He did not just stay with David, he ministered to him. The word "preside" which we earlier defined also means to be a pillar or support. A mentor is a supportive person who, despite the pains and problems, does not abandon, neglect or leave you alone in trying times.

Find a mentor who as a caregiver, exhibits qualities of listening, trust and rapport, provides friendship; validate your self-worth and serves as a confidant. A mentor is someone who is, above everything else, totally trustworthy. You can tell him or her things that you may not want others to know. A mentor is accepting: the mentor understands that you have areas for improvement as well as strengths and is non-judgmental about mistakes. A mentor shares his or her own personal life experiences and stories to help you booster your level of confidence to know that no matter how difficult your struggle is, you can also make it through.

Everyone of us sometimes has a need for affection and affirmation. That is what the mentor pours out. This affection is non sexual and non provocative; it is a cleansing stream for troubled waters. The mentor helps us see that though we are in troubled water, it will definitely stay calm after now. ***The good mentor communicates hope and optimism.*** Lasley argues that the crucial characteristic of mentors is the ability to communicate their belief that a person is capable of transcending present challenges and of accomplishing great things in the future.[14] Good mentor capitalize on opportunities to affirm the human potential of their mentees. They do so in private conversations and in public settings. Mentors are "*... tremendously important. We need mentors at all levels... These are people who support what you do and don't tell you what to do. With this sort of relationship, (you) can be open to criticism.*"[15] Have you watched the cartoon series of *Lion King?* When Scar killed Mofasa, the father of Simba because he wanted to be the king, Simba was unfortunately accused of murder; an act he did not commit. To save his life he ran away from pride land into the unknown. As a cub, he was faced with danger and uncertainty. It took Pumba: a pig and Timon: a Lizard to build strength and courage in Simba with the motto: *Akuno matata:* no worries or no problems. Pumba and Timon mentored Simba, talked out the Lion king in him into manifestation and supported his return to takeover the pride land.

A mentor can assist you with personal development, provide a forum for exploring personal/professional dilemmas whether it is being more effective at meetings, having better time management or building self-esteem, your mentor is there to help you with ideas. He can also be a sounding board while you talk, a contagious encourager in touch times. You need a mentor who takes genuine interest in you and what you are trying to achieve. He or she will share in your hopes and fears, your achievements and disappointments. "*A great mentor has a knack for making us think we are better than we think we are. They force us to have a good opinion of ourselves, let us know they believe in us. They make us get more out of ourselves, and once we learn how good we really are, we never settle for anything less than our very best.*"[16]

It is important to choose a mentor whose goals are similar to your own, one whose dream matches your dream, one who believes in your person and seeks to help you achieve your potential. Sometimes in this direction, it is important to find someone who is on the same career path. Choose a mentor who has time to give to you. Likewise, you must find the time to participate. As the one who will benefit most, you must make the initial step in establishing contact with a potential mentor. You must also work hard to maintain the relationship. You should bring trustworthiness and the ability to keep confidences to the mentoring relationship. Mentored relationships benefit when the mentee approaches the mentoring with openness, honesty, introspection, realistic expectations, accountability, and the ability to admit mistakes and share failures. The mentor asks relevant, searching, non-threatening questions to allow the mentee to discover the "answers" for himself or herself.

Tiger Woods had a mentor in his Father who died on May 4th 2006 at the age of 74 after a long fight with cancer. Earl Woods had inspired and moulded his son Eldrick into the golfing legend known as Tiger Woods. Earl Woods died in his Cypress, California, home where he and his Thai wife Kultida raised their famous son, who by the age of 30 had achieved 12 major titles. Tiger said of his father in his website; "My dad was my best friend and greatest role model, and I will miss him deeply. I'm overwhelmed when I think of all of the great things he accomplished in his life. He was an amazing dad, coach, mentor, soldier, husband and friend. "I wouldn't be where I am today without him, and I'm honoured to continue his legacy of sharing and caring," he said.[17]

Find a mentor who is successful. Birds of a feather flock together, therefore find a mentor who is successful. A mentor who believes that nothing is impossible will help not just aim for the stars, but also reach them. You cannot grow beyond the personal influences you allow into your life. Pastor Bob Shank of South Coast Community Church, California defines mentoring as a transfer of wisdom from one person to another. Mentoring is purposeful, intentional, and planned transfer of wisdom based on one's life experiences rather than through knowledge of systems or behavioural techniques.[18] Good mentors share their own struggles and frustrations and how they overcame them. And always, they do so in a genuine and caring way that engenders trust. A mentor "walks his talk", knows the way, shows the way and provides inspiration through their very being. A mentor is someone who we aspire to become. In fact, the mentor has qualities/skills we want for ourselves. So, a mentor must be successful to be able to advise and guide the protégée. Success in my definition does not have to do with material acquisitions rather; it is self-fulfillment and attainment in a chosen field of life. The mentor helps one to see possibilities by bringing to life the qualities we aspire for ourselves.

Therefore, identify someone you admire and respect, your daddy, uncle, school teacher, lecturer, pastor, deacon or whoever and deliberately decide to tap something worthwhile from that life. You can choose someone from your own place of employment or outside it or both. Some people have more than one mentor. These ones are "serial mentors," those with whom you have a short-term relationship, one after the other; it works well for some people.

Decide what you need in a mentor -- what skills you would like to develop with your mentor's assistance. Consider your goals in choosing a mentor. Think about what characteristics you are looking for in a mentor.[19] A mentor wants to work with someone he or she can respect. He or she may even desire to mold the protégé in his or her own image, which is fine as long as the mentor is not too obsessive. They will offer you advice and guidance in getting ahead in the world, and also give you encouragement and even push you when you need a gentle shove. It is also important to remember that not all mentoring occurs through face-to-face interaction; it can also take place through other media such as telephone conversations and email.

Mentoring is when one person, the mentor, helps another the mentee, to transform their knowledge, work or overall thinking into definite success.[20] This knowledge and or overall thinking might also be survival tips in a place of work, living or learning. A mentor might be a role model; someone you would like to model yourself after, but does not have to be. Minorities, under-represented, marginalized and persecuted in the workplace, may find it especially helpful to seek out mentors/role models of the same background so they can identify with the success of someone who has made it in a diverse workforce. The mentor may tend to give a lot more than you do to the relationship, so be sure to express regularly that you value and appreciate your mentor's guidance. The feeling of being needed and making a difference in a protégé's life will often be a rewarding payoff for the mentor, but do not be afraid to supplement that reward with a token gift, flowers, or by picking up the cheque when you share a meal. You could also send a note to the mentor's supervisor, praising his or her contribution to your professional growth.

Mentoring is a nurturing process in which a more experienced person, serving as a role model, teaches, sponsors, encourages, and befriends a less experienced person for the purpose of personal development. Mentoring is the art of helping and empowering others to shape their learning behaviours. Thinking back in your own life, who are the people who most positively influenced you: your parents, a specific teacher, perhaps your coach or a close friend? **The Golden Rule:** Do not choose a mentor that is within your reporting chain or whom you often work closely with. The golden rule gives you a big hint about what to look for — you want someone independent who you can bounce ideas off, discuss colleagues' behaviour with and talk to about leaving your job without fear of any comeback or hurting anyone's feelings. Whether or not your mentor is within the same company as you, depend on your own preferences. The mentor typically possesses the wisdom that only experience can provide.[21] Mentors are great off field assistants different from coaches. Coaches are side-line motivators who read the game and provide on the spot fresh strategies. So, there is also the need to have a coach for survival in hostile environment.

CHAPTER SEVEN:

FIND YOURSELF A COACH

Then David fled from Naioth in Ramah, and went and said to Jonathan, "What have I done? What is my iniquity, and what is my sin before your father, that he seeks my life?"2 So Jonathan said to him, "By no means! You shall not die! Indeed, my father will do nothing either great or small without first telling me. And why should my father hide this thing from me? It is not so!"3 Then David took an oath again, and said, "Your father certainly knows that I have found favor in your eyes, and he has said, 'Do not let Jonathan know this, lest he be grieved.' But truly, as the LORD lives and as your soul lives, there is but a step between me and death."4 So Jonathan said to David, "Whatever you yourself desire, I will do it for you."5 And David said to Jonathan, "Indeed tomorrow is the New Moon, and I should not fail to sit with the king to eat. But let me go, that I may hide in the field until the third day at evening.6 "If your father misses me at all, then say, 'David earnestly asked permission of me that he might run over to Bethlehem, his city, for there is a yearly sacrifice there for all the family.'7 "If he says thus: 'It is well,' your servant will be safe. But if he is very angry, then be sure that evil is determined by him.8 "Therefore you shall deal kindly with your servant, for you have brought your servant into a covenant of the LORD with you. Nevertheless, if there is iniquity in me, kill me yourself, for why should you bring me to your father?"9 ¶ But Jonathan said, "Far be it from you! For if I knew certainly that evil was determined by my father to come upon you, then would I not tell you?"10 Then David said to Jonathan, "Who will tell me, or what if your father answers you roughly?"11 And Jonathan said to David, "Come, and let us go out into the field." So both of them went out into the field. (1 Samuel 20: 1 – 11 NKJV).

David did not only rely on Samuel as a distant mentor; he also relied on someone on ground to survive his hostile environment. The person David struck an accord with was Jonathan to learn the tactics, get trained and taught the act of survival in the palace of Saul. Jonathan was a coach for David. **Survive in a hostile environment by finding yourself a coach.** While mentor might not have knowledge in your area of life, and might not even be on ground, a coach is a specialist in your area of survival and on ground. But suffice it to say that your mentor can also be your coach. Coaching *"is a process that enables learning and development to occur and thus performance to improve."[1]*

World-class athletes know it, so do opera divas, that you need a coach. Winners in every known profession know that without the right coach, they would not perform at their peak. In today's business and corporate world, in our living, learning and work environment, as organizations flatten or plateau, as work becomes pleasurable or under pressure, as production cycles hit hyper speed or crash, as management become friends or foe, as colleagues become ministers or mercenaries, as bosses become satans or saviour's, we need coaches who can help us become better professionals or business leaders. People proven to be outstanding in their careers had coaches on the sidelines or behind the scenes. **Every *successful person has a coach*.**[2] It is most likely there was a supportive and loving parent early in life, a teacher and later a career coach.

Throughout history, most of the great achievements and incredible comebacks, especially in sports, have been the results of individuals whose motivation to succeed was influenced by a coaches. In science, art, politics, sports, and business, there is a common trend of having a coach among those who achieve greatness. A coach is not necessarily a professional consultant or counselor, but someone within your organization, industry, profession, business or chosen career who becomes for you a trainer in professional ability, a tactician in plotting the course of office politics survival and a tutor in relational skills and professional excellence.

When we were toddlers, infants or even teenagers, we look to our parents and to other adults for guidance and help in learning how to survive in the world. In other words, we relied on others to teach us what we needed to know to get through life. We go through many changes as we grow to adulthood. We get bigger and stronger, develop relationships with others, go to school, and move on. No matter how much we grow or change, one aspect of our being remains the same. We all still look to those who have come before us to serve as good guides. As young professionals, we should seek out coaches who would lead us through the tough draws of corporate political intricacies, corporate intrigue, and pains to survive in our career. One way to survive is to find yourself a coach.

Find a coach who is a manager. [3]A manager is someone who has tact: skill in dealing with people or situations, someone with a delicate perception of the feelings of others, a guru in the act of management and a planner for unforeseen situations. David knew that in the palace of Saul,

Jonathan was the one with the tactics to make things happen. As heir apparent to the throne, Jonathan knew the politics of the palace, the power struggle, and the way things were done in the palace. If he was to survive in the intense palace jealousy, he needed someone who had the tactics/skills for survival. Jonathan became for David a coach. David knew that survival does not depend only on personal skills, but also on the tactician coach you have within your organization.

A coach who is a manager is one who is able to handle relationships, school you in the politics of power contest and content, able to point you to the dos and don'ts within your organization and where possible be your advocate in times of crisis. In order words, a professional, life or career coach teaches you how to climb in the political mesh and helps you develop a professional growth plan, and identifies resources to improve exposure. "... *To be successful a Coach requires knowledge and understanding of process as well as the variety of styles, skills and techniques that are appropriate to the context in which the coaching takes place*" [4]

A coach's skill helps you manage logistics and relationships. There are relationship traps you need a coach to survive; there are political hurdles you need a coach to scale; there are professional and academic problems through which you need a coach to help plot your success. A coach should have a working knowledge of your organizational culture, structure and processes. A coach knows the people dynamics, the strengths and weaknesses of the management team because he or she is a part of the structure. A coach is a manager of resolution. Coaches can help less resourceful individuals who are not "getting along" with boss, colleagues or management to "see things differently". This helps us to see that there are many more options than we ever imagined for getting what we really want when we are in conflict with one another. **A coach helps us manage our difficult boss, our troublesome husband, wife, child, education, business or whatever creates your hostile environment.** Difficult bosses can be a challenge to deal with. The coach helps us learn effective ways of communicating with our boss and meeting his/her needs while meeting your own for more job satisfaction and amazing career growth!!

A coach is an insider. With inside information and knowledge, a coach does not work in *a small dark room* but can talk specifically without vagueness and generalities in speech. A good coach helps us remain objective during emotional events that cut through our office productivity and is able to steer a course that is true to facts and knowledge. Such a coach helps us to sort through the distractions in the work place to realize the consequential gains of our decision for peak performance under pressure. We need to be taught the vital strategies, principles and skills necessary to survive and excel in today's fast- paced, pressure packed world. A coach is a hand to lean on.

In a hostile environment, we need to develop the skills and flexibility in our organization's leadership. Such skills will enhance the longevity of our business in this forever-changing global environment. To successfully do this, a coach provides a range of techniques for us that will enhance productivity, build capability and generate innovation under tension. By so doing we optimize the human assets in us, capitalize on leadership potential and create potential followers at all levels of our organization. A coach helps us to understand ourselves and gain insight into the behaviors of others for greater success.

Similarly, since a hostile environment can cripple our imagination, a coach facilitates new ways of thinking and response that gives us a competitive advantage and a powerful edge against official persecution. This is because a coach assesses the current structure of hostility against a person and recommends solutions to address obstacles to achieving business or official fulfillment. The coach shows us how current management systems support or oppose our business/official strategies, so we can evolve other systems to facilitate future growth.

The coach guides and actively encourages a person in the development of relevant skills and attitudes for the future. The focus of the coach is on our ability to see beyond the hostility in operation now, to identify what we can be later, and then to work us towards achieving our goal of excellence. A coach knows our professional strengths and weaknesses and helps develop skills for success and a long-range career plan. In this vein, we and our coach should share the same professional experience. Where this is the case, it can foster our sense of belonging within the organization, help us navigate the company culture and politics, as well as let us realize who the organization's key players are.

In May of 2004, the University of Chicago hosted its 52nd annual management conference with the theme: *It is not enough to do good work.* The bottom line of the conference was that "Reputations flourish not simply because you do good work, but because people tell stories about your good work,"[5] Simply put, the more people talk about what you do well, the better your performance reviews, raises and bonuses will tend to be. That is especially true when others talk about your good work to people in different parts of the company. It seems that when that type of information crosses department boundaries, it is seen as significantly more credible and newsworthy, naturally boosting your reputation.

A coach helps to adopt strategic patterns of work and conduct that gives you positive attention. Imagine what you could create if you were just that much more valued by key decision makers. Imagine what you could accomplish if you were listened to just a little more closely by those around you. Imagine the impact you could have if you were able to be just that much more influential. It won't happen overnight. But one thing is clear: You need to put the proper focus, structures, and accountabilities in place in order for such improvements to happen.

We need a coach to work through career and workplace problems. A coach does provide a fresh perspective, a new way of looking at a problem or issue. We can bounce ideas off our coach. Look for a coach who facilitates your decision-making process by suggesting what to do. While a mentor gives general advice, a coach tells us specifically what to do in a specific situation. A coach opens our eyes to see what we are doing and make simple adjustments that can save our months and years of trial and error. With a tactical coach versed in professional culture, you can survive hostile environments.

Find a coach who is a motivator.[6] A motivator is a person who equips others, instructs someone to educate, exercise and use their potentials to the fullest. In other words, a motivator helps you to grow. David was sad over the occurrences in the palace, but Jonathan became a source of strength and motivation for David in a time of crisis for survival. When things are tough, a coach still believes in you; when we are down and out, a coach knows how to bring out the best in us. A coach inspires, stimulates, informs, and encourages us that things are not yet over even in rough times. A coach trains us to realize who we are. Jonathan stood with David by reminding him of the fact that he was still the anointed of the Lord. Our coach should be an objective person with special knowledge and skills who understands our desires and needs while helping us to use our very best qualities and resources most effectively. No matter the tension our hostile environment generates, there is still ability in us to succeed.

A coach trains us to reconsider previously discounted possibilities and to develop new ones. A coach is a person of a second chance. Using thought-provoking questions, comments, role-playing, and a variety of other techniques, a coach helps us break out of the rut of indecision. "Coaches unlock a person's potential to maximize their own performance. It is helping them to learn rather than teaching them' says Timothy

Gallwey.[7] In fact, most people who hire coaches are already very successful. Yet in their success, they realize they can be even more successful, if they just make a few adjustments in their lives. A coach helps you to do exactly that. A coach has a set agenda to reinforce or change skills and behaviors. The coach has objective/goals for each discussion.

Mentoring and coaching are about development and helping someone to make the most of their talents, skills, jobs and career at a professional or personal level. There is a degree of overlap between the two roles.[8] However, a mentor might not be someone with direct experience in your career, but with coaching, direct experience in the same occupational area is necessary. However, suffice it to say that there are some persons whose mentors are also their coaches. According to Eric Parsloe, *"Coaching is directly concerned with the immediate improvement of performance and development of skills by a form of tutoring or instruction. Mentoring is always concerned with the longer term acquisition of skills in a developing career by a form of advising and counseling."*[9]

A coach trains someone in achieving the impossible. The coach makes us know that **just because it is not easy, does not mean it's impossible.** Know this: not being able to do something is quite different from not knowing how to do it. People who have been coached and who understand this distinction use it regularly. They have learned to see that the things that tend to give them the most trouble in work (and in life) are not things they are unable to do, but things they just have not learned to do well yet. A coach brings the power of awareness that very few things will stay impossible for long if you approach them as opportunities to learn something new and different.

In life, coaching is about making progress happen. As such, our professional success is determined by our ability to make good things happen sooner or later. Motivation is also about getting a clear vision of what we want to do, how we are going to do it, and when we are going to get it done. That is why working with a life coach makes sense. It is about future success. Sure, one might have made mistakes; it is what we learn (or do not learn) from those mistakes that matters most. Looking back at the challenges one has faced and overcome gives ones life a spark.

Some of us are suffering in hostile environments because we have no income of our own. How can you remain there destroyed by thoughts, pegged in by anxiety? Look within and find a coach to impart something into your life. Some of us are suffering professionally in a hostile environment because we do not have adequate qualifications or certificate to back up our practical knowledge of what we do. Find a coach. Idowu Akinrolabu was a graduate of geology until he was struck with Guillen barren syndrome: a disease that attacks the central nervous systems and leaves it victims completely paralyzed. He lost all movements in his body except his head. Depending on people was not easy as people began to complain. Determined to live he discovered something called mouth painting. He paid for a coach. Today Idowu has won several international Arts Awards and travel for international exhibitions. He has been able to care for himself and even his family.[10]

There is something visibly noticeable about the successful coach. They have what we call "Spark". Basically, this means that they are upbeat, are naturally positive, enjoy working with people, have a lot to give, have a sparkle in their eye and naturally turn others on. Not everyone has the Spark. Find a coach who has a spark, carries an aura of confidence and distils an air of courage. Coaching is a process that requires that the coach be sensitive, able to feel our energy/mood, able to distinguish subtleties, able to feel the information rather than having to acquire it, able to sense the truth about what's being said and able to guess well. Part of the process of survival in a hostile environment is to have a successful coach who is sensitive one in order for one's natural perceptive ability to develop.

A coach motivates us to realize that patience and persistence work hand-in-hand. Most people understand that just because something has not happened yet does not mean it would not ever happen. But people who have been coached tend to realize that some of the best opportunities are the ones they create for themselves. So in addition to learning how to take specific, targeted, and measurable steps forward, we should also come to understand that tenacity goes a long way to help make good things happen sooner.

A good coach plants seeds, but it takes more than just wishing for those seeds to flower. The good coach would help to achieve greatness knowing that it also takes time for nurturing and a bit of pruning too. But how beautiful can those flowers be when they finally do come into bloom! Coaches impact structures and language to address issues, challenges and opportunities facing you. Though on a longer term, it is about people learning to better help themselves – to create their own enduring value.

A good coach creates a supportive environment to challenge one to develop critical thinking skills, ideas and behaviors. While the strength of mentoring lies in the mentor's specific knowledge and wisdom, in coaching it lies in the facilitation and development of a person's personal and professional qualities.

Find a coach who is a master. A master is someone versed with a body of information, a master in his or her field, in fact a coach tutor is a professor of business, life or career issues. David knew that though he was in the palace, there was someone who had the palace not as a job but as a home. Jonathan was a master of royal business and politics, a child of the palace and a royalty in every right. It is true that birds of a feather flock together. Jonathan was a coach for David who was versed in royal relationship skills and intrigues. It was this knowledge that would help David survive.

The import of such knowledge is that our coach should be an accomplished professional in our field. You cannot give out what you do not have, so let us associate with a coach who can impact our life with knowledge.[11] The foundational block of survival in a hostile environment is knowledge of your context, sport, craft, or corporate game-playing. A competent coach is both a master and a student of the game, always seeking insights and a greater depth of understanding. A coach has a wealth of knowledge and has capsulated it for practical application. <u>The career advantage for you is not having to learn or reconstruct everything from the ground up. You can borrow from an existing body of knowledge. Solicit insight, stand on the shoulders of others, and get a head start.</u> The knowledge of a coach can eliminate trial and error, as well as identify critical principles.

A coach is a teacher of life success. Successful coaching is primarily conversation-based. The most successful coach finds that the give-and-take, back-and-forth flow of ideas, concepts, feelings, information, reality, wants, values and priorities, occurs effortlessly between them and the coached. A great coach encourages us to say things we have never said before. A competent coach brings a perspective gained over time through an increase of knowledge, practical experiences, analysis of information, and a synthesis of trends into our lives. Taking advantage of a coach's perspective allows another picture into our horizon that releases the genius in us.[12] Thus, we ascend into a plain where we separate hostility issues from personality issues, select a survival path over an immediate clique patronage, and effectively reach our ultimate goal.

A masterful coach is a person of alternative action. There are always alternatives to accomplish our goals; a coach provides insight on the skills of the "competition" we face.[13] In his or her role as a master, a coach guides on ways to stay focused and achieve objectives efficiently. A good coach has a wide, efficient and effective information network. His or her scope is broad, and he or she has feeders for detailed information within a professional or business circle.[14]

Effective coaches develop networks of contacts so they can get information when needed. They know sources that are reliable and can quickly do "reasonableness" check on information received. By being our confidant and independent sounding board, a coach makes us more aware of our opinions of others and helps us hear what we may be saying to others without realizing it. Through logic and common sense, a coach guides you to think through and analyze the steps you take and the decisions you make in determining the merits of a particular pattern of action. In reviewing your insights and observations from work of life, a coach works with you to frame your location, see what is in your way, and crystallize how you should move forward. A coach helps you explore alternatives to victory.

Having a coach would keep you on track, make you more accountable, and keep you constantly progressing forward so you actually see the results you want rather than just wishing for them. In both coaching and mentoring one-to-one focus and attention are key. "You can, in a one-to-one, focus on intra-personal issues to a far deeper level than in group environments which can only look at the superficial." A coach is your minister for survival affairs. I love the cartoon "Chicken Run"; a Dream works Pictures production. Each time there was a drop in egg production Mrs. Tweedy the farm owner would assemble all the birds and take an invention of each bird's egg production. Any one whose production had dropped was immediately killed. This would make all the birds sorrowful. However, Mrs. Tweedy nursed an idea of making chicken pies so she began to assemble her machines. With this in progress the birds began to plan chicken run, but how would they escape since the farm was fenced and guarded by ferocious dogs? One day, a cock "Rocky" flew into the farm, that was how Ginger; one of the birds asked Rocky to teach them how to fly. As hope dimmed after many days of practice without success, Ginger thought of a Fowler; a three star medal, formerly a member of the British Royal Air force. Ginger, felt it was possible to build a machine to escape like one of those that Fowler flew in the Air force. It was an alternative action. They built a wooden aircraft propelled by simultaneous pedaling. It worked and the chickens escaped thanks to Coach Ginger. With a good coach you can achieve the impossible in your profession or career.

Press briefs about Coaching: [15]

- **Fortune Magazine** ..."In a recent study, training alone improved leadership skill by 22%. When combined with Executive Coaching, improvement jumps to 77%."

- **The Chicago Tribune** ..."Who exactly seeks out a coach? Winners who want more out of life."

- **The Harvard Business Review** ..."The goal of coaching is the goal of good management— to make the most of an organization's valuable resources."

- **Time Magazine** ..."Coaching is an action-oriented partnership that, unlike psychotherapy, which delves into patterns of the past, concentrates on where you are today and how to reach your goals."

- **The Business Journal** ... "A coach is part advisor, part sounding board, part cheerleader, part manager, and part strategist ... The coach prods the client to keep to the action plan."

- **Newsweek Magazine** ... "Part consultant, part motivational speaker... coaches work with managers, entrepreneurs, and just plain folks, helping them define and achieve their goals."

- **Money Magazine...** "The benefits of coaching appear to win over even the most cynical of clients within just a few weeks."

- **The Wall Street Journal** ... "THE EXECUTIVE says his fears disappeared when his supervisor described the proposed coaching as an opportunity 'to get some outside points of view on what we do'."

- **CNN.com** ... "Once used to bolster troubled staffers, coaching now is part of the standard development training for elite executives and talented up-and-comers."

- **Business Week** ... "As for coaching, having someone listen to you and encourage you, and break everything down into easy concrete steps is rather nice."

- **The New York Times on the Web** ... "[Coaches] are becoming popular with professionals and entrepreneurs seeking to improve their performance in business, to better their relationships, and to help set goals."

An important part of the success strategy that coaches teach is the need to keep your vision alive. A vision is what empowers you to keep on keeping on even when the circumstances are not right. This is because you know what you want to achieve and you do not intend to mess it up.

CHAPTER EIGHT:

KEEP YOUR DREAM ALIVE.

Now David came to Nob, to Ahimelech the priest. And Ahimelech was afraid when he met David, and said to him, "Why are you alone, and no one is with you?" David said to Ahimelech, "The king has charged me with a matter, and said to me, 'Do not let anyone know anything about the business on which I send you, or what I have commanded you.' And I have directed my young men to such and such a place.3 "Now therefore, what have you on hand? Give me five loaves of bread in my hand, or whatever can be found."4 And the priest answered David and said, "There is no common bread on hand; but there is holy bread, if the young men have at least kept themselves from women."5 Then David answered the priest, and said to him, "Truly, women have been kept from us about three days since I came out. And the vessels of the young men are holy, and the bread is in effect common, even though it was sanctified in the vessel this day."6 So the priest gave him holy bread; for there was no bread there but the showbread which had been taken from before the LORD, in order to put hot bread in its place on the day when it was taken away.7 Now a certain man of the servants of Saul was there that day, detained before the LORD. And his name was Doeg, an Edomite, the chief of the herdsmen who belonged to Saul.8 And David said to Ahimelech, "Is there not here on hand a spear or a sword? For I have brought neither my sword nor my weapons with me, because the king's business required haste."9 So the priest said, "The sword of Goliath the Philistine, whom you killed in the Valley of Elah, there it is, wrapped in a cloth behind the ephod. If you will take that, take it For there is no other except that one here." And David said, "There is none like it; give it to me." (1Samuel 21: 1 – 9 NKJV).

A Hostile environment can be a Workplace, a home, an academic institution or any place of living, work and learning. It is one where people cannot do their best work or be most productive due to conditions that imprison their potential or threaten their physical safety and welfare. In essence, a hostile environment is hostile to our natural humanity. The threats that such an environment poses include hostility toward the company's productivity, which directly impacts on profits in a negative way. People who are unhappy, unhealthy or angry do not work hard.

A hostile workplace is the result of intimidation and suppression of people's natural ability to express themselves since it does not promote creativity and vitality. Hostile workplaces are deadly to productivity, unhealthy to prosperity and potentially deadly - to the people who work in them. This is because the leads to acts of violence against persons or property, threats, intimidation, harassment, or other inappropriate, disruptive behaviours cause fear for personal safety in that hostile environment. Hostile environments can affect or involve employees, visitors, contractors, and other non-related family members.

David had found himself caught up in a hostile environment for a job he was both called and qualified to do. Having escaped from the death traps of Saul, he made an advance for his survival by keeping his focus on his dream. In a hostile environment keep your dream alive if you want to survive. A dream is an "ambition: a cherished desire; imaginative thoughts indulged in while awake; a state of mind characterized by abstraction and release from reality." [1]

A dream is a visionary creation of the imagination. Your dreams often contain valuable information that will help you to understand yourself and your world much better. Your dream defines your life. Chances are that if you have a job, you have a boss and colleague to work with. You might be favoured to work with nurturing and supportive bosses or colleagues; then, count yourself favoured. But there are some who are struggling like David to keep a work relationship that resembles a good day. Since bosses are only human, a "perfect" boss is as impossible to imagine as a "perfect" person. Therefore if you are caught up in the mesh of hostility to survive, keep your dream alive. A hostile environment could possibly happen to anyone, anywhere. When confronted with any, be ready to survive beyond any event. To survive means to remain alive; to live. Survival is taking any given circumstance, accepting it, and trying to improve it, while sustaining your life until you can get out of the situation. **And most importantly, survival is a state of mind.**

Keep your dreams alive with your integrity. Integrity comprises the personal inner sense of "wholeness" deriving from honesty and consistent uprightness of character. The etymology of the word relates it to the Latin adjective *integer* (bringing several separate elements into a whole, complete). Integrity connotes strength and stability.[2] It means taking the high road by practicing the highest business ethics and professional standards.

Demonstrating integrity in a hostile environment shows completeness and soundness in our character and in our person.

Cheshire Calhoun argues that integrity is primarily a social virtue, one that is defined by a person's relations to others.[3] The social character of integrity is, Calhoun claims, a matter of a person's proper regard for his or her own best judgement. Persons of integrity do not just act consistently with their endorsements; they stand for something: they stand up for their best judgment within a community of people trying to discover what in life is worth doing. As she puts it:

> Persons of integrity treat their own endorsements as ones that matter, or ought to matter, to fellow deliberators. (They do not go around to) Absent a special sort of story, lying about one's views, concealing them, recanting them under pressure, selling them out for rewards or to avoid penalties, and pandering to what one regards as the bad views of others, all indicate a failure to regard one's own judgment as one that should matter to others.[4]

There were two things that David did which border on integrity. One is what we should not do while the other is what we should in a hostile environment as we fight for survival. When David came to Nod and Ahimelech the Priest went out to meet him, David told a lie to Ahimelech that he was on a royal errand. That was a lie, which David cropped up to hide the harassment against him and the fact that he had left the palace. However, one thing that is worthy of emulation is that, even in the harassments David and his men had kept themselves from sexual immorality. The exact word used is "consecration."

In a hostile environment we should not lie to protect ourself. As far as the psychology of the unconscious is concerned, lying is a fact of life. When you tell a lie you make a deliberate, conscious effort to deceive someone, and that deception, at its psychological core, is in itself an act of aggression. The aggression derives from a belief that someone has failed you in some way, and, in that failure, you feel a threat to the defenses you use to prop up a fabricated sense of invulnerability. The greatest witness on the job is to be personally pleasant and undeniably productive. Unfortunately, we grow up feeling obligated to share our faith rather than to allow people to observe it by our professional integrity.

A survey carried out by *Human Resource Magazine* found out that one in five workers admit to telling lies at work. According to another survey on honesty in the workplace, 19 percent of workers admit they tell lies at the office at least once a week, and 15 percent say they' have been caught in a lie at work.[5] These are some common lies. "I' have been out sick, sure, I'll call you right back, I have another call to take, I will call you right back, I never got your email, I don't know what happened." Hinman says it may be a cliché, but honesty is the best policy, especially at work.[6] Which ones have you used? More than 2,000 people were interviewed for the survey. One in four managers also said they have fired an employee for being dishonest, so be careful when telling those tell tales at work.

Kate DuBose Tomassi has identified the Most Common Resume Lies that can nail you in a work environment. Some of these are:[7]

- **Lying about getting a degree:** Indeed, you had every intention of finishing up that Public Administration course. That you enrolled in a course, or finished the course work without the project does not mean you can claim you got it. Is the degree awarded to you by the institution?
- **Playing with dates to hide employment gaps.** The reasons are myriad: hiding being fired, a period of job hopping or even an embarrassing prison stay. Some women hid their true biological status because they fear it will be difficult to re-enter the workplace after starting a family.
- **Exaggerating numbers**: Want to claim you made your previous employer a million dollars last year? That will look impressive. But remember that your new boss will expect you to deliver the same for him.
- **Inflating titles:** You would have been promoted to vice president of sales at your prior job if the company had truly realized your value as an employee, right? So why not just anoint yourself with the title you deserved? Wrong.

David told a lie to Ahimelech which led to the death of 85 priests (cf: 1 Samuel 22: 1 – 23). In a hostile environment, your lies can put your helpers into trouble because there are those who would genuinely wish to lend you support. Lying carries dire consequences in a hostile environment. Lying is theft. When you tell me something which I take to be true and as a result I invest my time, or my money, or even my care, you have stolen these things from me because you obtained them with false information.

Lying creates inequality. You also do not like being lied to, I have never known anyone who wanted to be deceived, you have acted as if there were two classes of humans: you, with the right to lie, and everyone else, who must be truthful to you so that you too will not lose your way. Lying treats people as means to the end you wish to accomplish and not as ends in themselves. Lying is fraud. Lying one of those rare areas in which the moral rulebook and the legal one overlap each other quite neatly. Fraud is defined as an intentional falsehood on which another relies to his detriment. A fraud is a lie writ large, often in a financial context, where the damage to me is quantifiable in money. Even those lies which the law does not define as fraud tend to fit the same definition: a knowing false utterance indirectly brings harm, and does. The only differences are of degree, for example, when we cannot assess the loss in money.

The basic tenet that lying is wrong seems to be universal to all cultures, probably because humans are social animals. To live together in a society, we must tell the truth to each other about such basic matters as sources of food or of danger. Sissela Bok says: *"A society, then, whose members were unable to distinguish truthful messages from deceptive ones, would collapse. But even before such a general collapse, individual choice and survival would be imperiled. The search for food and shelter could depend on no expectations from others."* [8]

Lies only work when no one bothers to research them; lies are poisons that gradually eat up the fabric of everything around it. They eat up your conscience, courage, commitment and colour. Bok says "[F]ew lies, are solitary ones. The first lie 'must be thatched with another or it will rain through.' More and more lies may come to be needed; the liar always has more mending to do. And the strains on him become greater each time... After the first lies, moreover, others can come more easily. Psychological barriers wear down; lies seem more necessary, less reprehensible; the ability to make moral distinctions can coarsen..." [9] One of my favourite cartoon films is the story of Pinocchio: the wooden puppet that really wanted to become a boy. Having been touched by a supernatural fairy mother, Pinocchio became almost human. However, in the story of its incarnation Pinocchio lied, and the more he lied the more his wooden nose grew longer. It was only when he decided to start telling the truth that he really became a real boy with real human flesh. Beloved, lies keep you from being the real you. Until you tell the truth, you are not who you claim to be.

Some people say we are all liars. This was the excuse some made for Bill Clinton lying about Monica Lewinsky: that the press had no right to inquire into his private life. There is always an opportunity to lie in our hostile environments, but let us allow integrity to rule our lives. You must learn that you have emotions both pleasant and unpleasant and learn to recognize and name them. You must learn that you have been using some very clever unconscious or conscious psychological defenses to push out of awareness all the unpleasant and frightening emotions which traumatize you in the hostile environment. You must learn that the past essentially continues to live in the present; because every lie you tell today awaits clarification tomorrow. Therefore, make a conscious effort to resist the temptation to fall into old defensive lying patterns; train yourself to act with new and different behaviours. [10]

Keep your dreams alive with your instincts. An instinct is an inborn pattern of behaviour often responsive to specific stimuli, Instinct is the word used to describe inherent dispositions towards particular actions. Instincts are generally inherent pattern of responses or reactions to certain kinds of situations. In humans, they are most easily observed in responses to emotions and bodily functions. Instincts generally serve to set in motion mechanisms that evoke an organism to action. The particular actions performed may be influenced by learning, environments, and natural principles.[11] An instinct is an agent which performs blindly and ignorantly a work of intelligence and knowledge. Sir W. Hamilton. It is a natural inward impulse; unconscious, involuntary, or unreasoning prompting to any mode of action. An instinct is an inherited tendency to general forms of response to given situations; the specific response is almost always a combination of inherited tendency with acquired modifications.[12]

While David was there before Ahimelech the priest receiving bread and even sword, Doeg the Edomite, Chief shepherd of Saul was there. Yet, instinct could not tell David that this was already a dangerous game. In a hostile environment you do not need to be very knowledgeable to survive. A bit of native intelligence and situation management helps you to decode what would happen after now. Doeg as a chief shepherd of Saul was a threat, a potential danger, and one who would want to put himself in Saul's good book by reporting what he saw. How could David have left off recognizing this threat called Doeg. The name Doeg means "anxiety. He might have been among those who felt slighted with the exaltation of David and his action of just stalking there in quietness gives us a clue to recognizing threats in our hostile environment.

Predicting when an individual might be "a risk factor" to create a hostile environment act is difficult but sometimes obvious. Be aware of situations and people who might harm you. Do not ignore certain warnings about particular people or social settings. Trust your own instincts about possible danger. The following are warning indicators of potential workplace hostility:

- When a person becomes sarcastic, irritable, or of moody behaviour;
- When a person becomes apathetic and/or inconsistent with work performance;
- When a person is prone to making direct or veiled threats in a place;
- When a person becomes aggressive and manifests antisocial behaviour towards others;
- When a person over-reacts to discussions about a boss, policies or performance appraisals;
- When a person becomes touchy in relationships with other workers. "This place is all messed up; somebody should pay for what goes on here;"
- When a person has obsessive involvement and/or emotional attachment to job;
- When a person has numerous conflicts with customers, co-workers, or supervisors;
- When a person makes statement about direct or veiled threats of harm. "This place is all messed up; I would like to torch it;"
- When a person brings a weapon to the workplace (unless necessary for the job); making inappropriate references to guns, or making idle threats about using a weapon to harm someone;
- When a person makes statements showing fascination with incidents of workplace violence, statements indicating approval of the use of violence to resolve a problem, or statements indicating identification with perpetrators of workplace homicides. "If I do not get some respect here, there is going to be a problem;"
- When a person makes statements indicating desperation (over family, financial, and other personal problems) to the point of contemplating suicide. "You have been treating me this way for years. I am going to get you even if it destroys me;"

- When a person engages in substance abuse;
- When a person shows extreme changes in normal behaviors.

There are warning signs that an environment can become hostile. Do not wait for it to reach a point where they suddenly burst. Like Doeg, when a person exhibits emotional instability or violent behaviour, signs of extreme stress, undergoes profound personality changes, feels victimized by supervisors or the entire organization, makes threats or alludes to acts of workplace violence, exhibits signs of extreme paranoia or depression, displays behaviour inappropriate to the situation at hand, exhibits signs of drug or alcohol abuse, is involved in a troubled, work- related romantic situation, be careful, look very well and do not lay out your cards in the presence of these people.

Keep your dreams alive with your insights. Insight is another word for vision. Insight is a vivid mental image of the person you are waiting to manifest. In other words, insight is an inner sight into your purpose and passion for life. Insight is the ability to see; it helps our imagination, quickens the formation of a mental image of something that is not perceived as real and is not present to the physical senses. A powerful insight provides us in the hostile environment with a possibility that lies ahead. In fact, a compelling insight is a word picture of what one intends ultimately to become - which may be five, ten, or fifteen years in the future.

Insight is a present-tense statement that communicates where we believe we will be within a stated time period, and it is a description of our desired 'world', always far greater than any hostile environment in which we work, live or learn. When David held the sword of Goliath in his hands he said "there is none like it." David saw inside of him the warrior God made him to be, the deliverer God called him to be, the shepherd who defends the flock and the anointed king over Israel. In David's mind he could still hear the song of the women, the roar of the entire army of Israel and the celebration when he killed Goliath. Even in the present hostility he faced with Saul, he could still see the purpose of his life manifesting; the anointed king of Israel. David then could see that no matter what the present situation was he was anointed for the job.

In a hostile environment keep your dreams alive by remembering the vision, the insight that brought you to where you are. You are not in that place by chance: there is a reason heaven allowed you into that school, work or home. Therefore, do not expect to quit until you have fulfilled your destiny. Heaven brought you there by a grand design. In a hostile environment do not cease to remember how you got to where you are. Know that God anointed and picked you specially for that place where it appears hell has gone lose.

Insight means seeing beyond the obvious - seeing the unseen. The environment might be hostile: do not forget the vision to be the Chairman and chief executive in that place. The place might be tough; life might be rough; it might appear that you are living dangerously; your files are filled with queries; your work is subjected to extraordinary scrutiny; your vote, leave or promotion is never approved: do not forget the vision. In the hostile environment, there is something that cannot be denied, and that is that you have an ability to make success happen. That ability to make success happen was what qualified you and stood you out to get the job you are doing. David took hold of the sword of Goliath and said there is none like it. Look back into your work, learning or living environment: no matter how hostile, you will find a reminder of what you have achieved. Allow that mile post to drive you on. Do not expect to be appreciated, do not expect a letter of commendation, and zero your mind to get the worker of the month or year award. These things might be denied you, but they are only momentarily. Your quality will speak for you at the right moment. Do not forget the vision.

The sword of Goliath that David asked for was a symbol of personal development. In a hostile environment, you cannot climb the corporate ladder beyond what you have. Seek to develop yourself through acquisition of more or better professional qualifications and certificates. It might take them ten years to recognize it, but one day they will. So, learn to broaden your perspective, to question the obvious, to reach beyond where your aggressors are, and to follow your dream. If you are to survive, follow your insight in spite of obstacles or non-believers. The only requirement is a strong desire to grow and expand beyond where you are.

Despite the hostile environment, know that you still have a future. Do not become so tied up with the present routine of hostility you are in, like sorting out your manager's work, receiving threats of death, non-appreciation and even verbal abuses. Like David, be aware of what you are good at, what you enjoy, and power your purpose to a great height. Have a belief that your contribution is vital, no matter what you do. Take ownership for your own development. REMEMBER: Vision without action is merely a dream. - Action without vision is a waste of time. *"Dream as if you'll live forever. Live as if you'll die today."* James Dean.

Survival in a hostile environment that keeps your dream or insight alive only comes from a combination of vision and strategy. Henry Ford, for example, not only had a vision of an America reshaped by affordable automobiles, but also a highly successful strategy built around mass production and mass marketing. Throughout history, successful business or career ventures – from Ted Turner's CNN to Steve Case's America On Line to Bill Gates' Microsoft to Oprah Winfrey's inspirational empire – have all been made possible by the combination of vision and strategy, of insight and execution. Social and religious leaders such as Arch Bishop Ola Makinde, Professor Yusuf Ameh Obaje, Gani Fawehimi, Olisah Agbakoba, Madam Tinubu, Princess Idia and Martin Luther King Jr. had the same combination – an inspiring vision of what society could be, and strategies based on civil disobedience for helping make that vision a reality.

Vision and strategy are both required for survival in a hostile environment. To get the most out of your hostile environment, ask yourself if you have both a vision and a strategy. Think about your vision for your future – Do you really know what you have achieved and where you wish to make progress? Have you really thought about who you want to become? Know that **where you are heading for is better than where you are.** Remember:

"Real integrity is doing the right thing, knowing that nobody's going to know whether you did it or not." (Oprah Winfrey). Also, "Integrity is not a conditional word. It doesn't blow in the wind or change with the weather. It is your inner image of yourself…, (John D. MacDonald) people lack integrity because they fail to become mentally tough to cope with their hostility.

CHAPTER NINE:

DEVELOP MENTAL TOUGHNESS.

Then David arose and fled that day from before Saul, and went to Achish the king of Gath.11 And the servants of Achish said to him, "Is this not David the king of the land? Did they not sing of him to one another in dances, saying: 'Saul has slain his thousands and David his ten thousands'?"12 Now David took these words to heart, and was very much afraid of Achish the king of Gath.13 So he changed his behavior before them, feigned madness in their hands, scratched on the doors of the gate, and let his saliva fall down on his beard.14 Then Achish said to his servants, "Look, you see the man is insane. Why have you brought him to me?15 "Have I need of madmen, that you have brought this fellow to play the madman in my presence? Shall this fellow come into my house?" (1 Samuel 21: 10 – 15 NKJV).

In a hostile environment anything is possible, from death to destruction; character assassination to career to assassination; private gossips to position gambling, interesting groupings to influential gangsters; sexual tradeoffs to secret treaties. A hostile environment is a place for the survival of the fittest. However; we need motivation and attitude in the midst of the pressures we face.

Some of these pressures have to do with aligning with cliques and groups in the work place, school or institution to either fight our course or protect our interest. When confronted with these expected and sometimes unexpected factors, you are forced to rely upon your own resources for improvising needs and solving problems for yourself, If you want to survive in a hostile environment, you must ultimately decide to take care of yourself and not count on others.

David saw that the battle Saul declared against him had become tough and fierce. He decided ultimately to take his destiny into his own hands. Having received the sword of Goliath from Ahimelech the Priest, one thing was now paramount in David's mind - the will to live, and the courage to survive. David began to build up his mental stamina to cope with the stress, plan his next lines of actions and adopt strategies that would suit his survival plans. **Develop mental toughness: determine to survive in a hostile environment.**

According to Steve Fraser, Mental Toughness, by definition is "to be strong and resilient; able to withstand great strain without tearing or breaking."[1] Mental stamina is a passion to live and not expire. It is the ability to become toughened in your mind, and to refuse to pack up in the face of seemingly insurmountable obstacles. In the hostile environment, you face intimidation, physical abuses and hostility to your work and person, deprivation of rightful provisions and resources, evasion by colleagues, cold treatment and even bullying by your bosses. In all, determine not to throw in the towel. You must continually strive towards a goal of survival. Picture your goal in your mind and visualize yourself reaching it. A person with a stubborn strong will power can conquer many obstacles. Never give up your passion to live, because without any will to live, you will be lost in the wilderness.

Put on courage like a garment. David fled from the face of Saul. To flee (bârach) means to bolt away suddenly without prior preparation and arrangement, or to make haste to run away.[2] Remember, he who fights and runs away lives to fight another day. The attitude of David was not an escapist attitude to run away from the reality on ground. When you are caught up in a hostile environment, face up to the reality on the ground by knowing where you are. The attitude of David in suddenly fleeing without prior preparation or plan was not anti courage. When you get caught up in a hostile environment, survival hinges on mental toughness more than anything else.

The biggest obstacles in a hostile environment are psychological. These include: Fear of the unknown; stress over things that are beyond your control; anger at being in this situation; guilt over the errors you have made; but, it is important to recognize that these emotions are normal. However, it is necessary to point out that such feelings are potentially overwhelming. If you dwell on the negative, you become paralyzed, depressed, and indecisive. The negative emotions will crush your confidence. Instead of allowing fear and anxiety to become destructive, learn how to use those emotions as a positive force in fact, as motivation to keep going, to avoid being cavalier and leaving yourself vulnerable to the enemy, rise to the challenge.

In a hostile environment you need courage. Courage is the mental toughness of being able to create positive emotions upon command, enabling you to bring all your talent and skills to life in a moment. In this your brain will be your best asset but it could also be your most dangerous enemy. You will have to defeat negative thoughts of job termination, implication in fraud; even imaginations of harm. Therefore, control and master your fears. Courage is ability to shift mental processes and adopt a positive and optimistic attitude. Courage for survival allows you to work with the hostile environment by not allowing it to get inside you. As the situation gets nasty, people become more hostile; as camps and groups plan and adopt their strategy, as you are sidelined in the scheme of things, as you are deprived your rightful entitlements, recognize threats to your life and career; study the priority of influence of your aggressors; determine the severity of their hostility to your position, and toughen your mind to stay alive.

David ran when the threat was serious. It is courageous to run from harm to plan a better strategy for the battle. Know when to stay and when to run: Even under the most ideal circumstances, temporary exit from a place of harm is quite formidable. In survival in a hostile environment, learn to contend with the stressors of queries; learn to walk the rough terrain of negative office politics, and the variety of craftiness lurking somewhere within official assignments. Take the heat of verbal insults, endure the cold withdrawal and exclusion from social life, endure the rain of insults, cope with the winds of the unexpected, climb the mountains of ingratitude, walk the swamps of dirty office politics, the deserts of deprivation, insects of environmental antagonism, and other challenges awaiting you. There is a time to walk away from trouble. This reminds me of the book *Odenigbo* by Thomas Chigbo. Odenigbo was a local farmer and also a messenger in a white man's office. It happened that one day when he went to farm to check his traps unknowing to him one of them had caught a leopard which had been terrorizing the villagers. After battling with the beast for several hours, he was able to kill it and carried it to the village. By tradition, Odenighbo would become a high Chief greeted *Ogbu agu* (Killer of strong animal). As the ceremony for his confirmation was on the Osuofia of Okofia, a noted traditional ruler sent his men to capture Odenigbo and bring the carcass of the animal to this palace. Instead of putting up a resistance he followed them and later escaped from there to the shrine where he became untouchable.

Depending on how you handle the stress of your hostile environment, your surroundings can be either a source of motivation or a cause of extreme discomfort leading to injury, illness, or death. Always remember to keep your courage. Do not add any extra burden to yourself by falling into a destructive mental state like feeling self-pity or hopelessness. In a hostile environment courage helps you remember the important aspects of your life. Keep the image and do not allow the memory fade away. Think of your harassments as an opportunity to explore your potential. Your positive mental attitude will help you combat your survival enemies.

While under threat, the greatest intimidating tools remain loneliness, fatigue of job stress, pain of emotional drain, cold treatment by bosses or colleagues and fear. Any one or a combination of these can diminish your self-confidence or reduce your desire to struggle for life. All of these feelings are perfectly normal but are more severe and dangerous in hostile survival situations. By learning to identify them you will be able to control them instead of letting them control you. **Loneliness is a survival enemy that can hit you without warning**. It will strike you when you realize there is no person around who you can depend on while in your situation. Nowadays modern society barely gives us a chance to test our ability to adapt to silence, loss of support, and separation from others. Do not let loneliness gnaw at your positive attitude. Fight it by keeping busy, by singing, whistling, gathering data or doing anything else that will take your mind off the fact that you are alone. Also while in your survival situation, boredom or lack of interest might strike you. It must be cured to maintain a healthy survival attitude. Once again keep busy to keep your mind occupied.

Put off cliques like a garment. In a hostile environment due to fear of insecurity and uncertainty, we are prone to joining alliances and associations. David ran away from Saul and fled to Achish, King of Gath. Remember, Goliath was from Gath. Desperation made David to seek refuge in the camp of the enemy. The worst thing that can happen to you in a hostile environment is to join cliques and alliances. No matter how capable you are, when you join an alliance you are a late comer to it and would have to fight to keep your place. Whenever you join an alliance, you raise more enemies for yourself because there are those you are about to displace.

One component of mental toughness is a refusal to join any clique or alliance. The *Oxford English Dictionary* defines a clique as "a small group of people who spend time together and do not readily allow others to join them". A clique by its very definition excludes people and there are never any benefits in excluding your fellow employees. Do not join any allegiance because your chiefs will exploit you. In a hostile environment that is filled with intrigue, power play, cross carpeting and humiliation watch your associations. There are bosses within your institution, employment, company e.t.c who have a score to settle with one another. There are bosses who are disgruntled elements, seeking for a ground to plot a rebellion against the authority or another boss. These ones are quick to identify with you in your persecution and pretend as if they truly believe in your course.

They will only use you and dump you. Achish sent David to raid in the region of Israel among his own people. What a tragedy to find yourself as a tool to settle office war. Similarly, do not join any alliance because your colleagues will expose you. When you come into any alliance there is every likelihood that you would displace some persons from favour. Those in the camp, having known your potential, will feel threatened; they will expose you to the chiefs since they need favour too.

Cliques get in the way of effective relationship. People shut out of a group seldom talk to those on the inside. Similarly, those in a clique do not tap into the expertise of outsiders. In other words, if you have got cliques, your company is not as productive as it could be, and you have probably not getting full value from your employees. You have probably noticed that when given the chance, employees tend to congregate with people who are similar to them in age, race, education, and gender. Such clustering is known as homophily, or the tendency to seek out those who are similar. We all enjoy the camaraderie of like-minded people who share similar characteristics and interests. We understand that in every life situation, cliques are formed based on race, religion, economic class, work and children. In every imaginable situation, likes and dislikes, alliances and exclusions form. However, there are negative aspects with cliques. It is better to break out from clique environments.

- Cliques carry an aloof mystique. Move past the small, limited world of the clique. Organize regular social events with your workmates and invite everyone in your team.
- When you go for lunch, ask the people around if they would like to join you.
- Avoid taking lunch breaks with the same set of people every day.
- Take the time to get to know some of your lesser-known colleagues a little better.
- Build respect for people as individuals and not because of the group to which they belong. Be as inclusive of new employees as you can.
- Put yourself in their place and consider how daunting it would be to enter an environment dominated by an impenetrable clique of existing employees.

- Avoid making private jokes in front of people who are not included in your fun and games. Telling jokes about colleagues is never okay.
- Avoid passing on office gossip. Gossip quickly turns from speculation to misinformation, and can be hurtful and destructive. Requesting help and advice can be a great way of showing respect and appreciation towards your workmates.
- Build your self-confidence so that you are less dependent on the opinions and validation of others. Seek out mentoring or coaching services if needed.
- Do not be afraid of breaking away from a clique or of losing a perceived support network. Cliques can often be more about power and control than friendship, and ultimately, this is not the kind of support you need in your career. If you have a destructive clique in your workplace, consider approaching the people involved and letting them know how others feel about their behaviour. Remember, what goes around comes around, so whether you are part of the "in" crowd or not, take these tips to have a more cohesive team and a good working environment.

Put on camouflage like a garment. Camouflage is the method which allows an otherwise visible organism or object to remain indiscernible from the surrounding environment. Examples include a tiger's stripes and the battledress of a modern soldier. Camouflage is a form of deception. The word camouflage comes from the French word *"camoufler"* meaning 'to disguise'. [3]

There are essentially two approaches to camouflage - in both nature and human efforts - *disruptive camouflage* or *blending camouflage*. Disruptive camouflage produces its effect by breaking up and thereby concealing the structural lines of the object which it hides. An exact match with the environment's colors is much less important than the patterning of the regions of color themselves. Disruptive patterns are designed to counter in-built perceptual models. In humans these include the tendency to fill in gaps between aligned, or seemingly aligned, shapes to create 'whole' objects (closure and continuity). That overlapping, or appearing to overlap, is part of grouping shapes together (proximity grouping). That similar shape belong together, they are a coherent unit, while dissimilar shapes are parts of different units (similarity grouping) and so on. This is also called *high difference camouflage.*[4]

Blending camouflage is a more obvious approach. The camouflaged object is shielded by matching one or more of the following - the color, texture, shape, or pattern of other objects in the environment. In nature the copied objects tend to be non-edible and non-threatening. This camouflage is also called *high similarity camouflage* or *figure-ground blending.*[5]

To dream that you are in camouflage suggests that you are hiding your true self and feelings. You are hiding who you really are. When David saw the problem he was in, he changed his attitude. Camouflage your attitude in the hostile environment by becoming less predictable in actions and reactions. Let your utterances become less predictable, your socialization points and posts, the route through which you move in and out of work, the way you do your work, the manner of approach to your boss and the pattern of prosperity and comfort at your disposal. Hide who you are. Keep your joker to your chest.

When you are exposed to the elements of shame, disgrace, quarries, fear, intimidation, insults, deprivation and even physical attacks, get sheltered by changing your attitudes to become less predictable yet keeping true to your integrity and quality. Work late sometimes, do those jobs without asking questions, keep late to finish your task and meet your deadlines, stop the complaints and protests you are known for, refuse to fight where you where known to pick up a quarrel on issues, and even act the fool when your rights are trampled upon deliberately. As best you can, blend into your environment and do not give them an opportunity to totally interpret your strategy and activity of survival. Remember your positive frame of mind and keep your goal to live fresh in your mind. When you do this you are able to touch the lives of others who are also going through pains like you. Remember success in life does not depend on how happy you are, but how happy others are because of you. Think!

CHAPTER TEN:

BECOME A CITY OF REFUGE FOR OTHERS

David therefore departed from there and escaped to the cave of Adullam. And when his brothers and all his father's house heard it, they went down there to him. 2 And everyone who was in distress, everyone who was in debt, and everyone who was discontented gathered to him. So he became captain over them. And there were about four hundred men with him.3 Then David went from there to Mizpah of Moab; and he said to the king of Moab, "Please let my father and mother come here with you, till I know what God will do for me."4 So he brought them before the king of Moab, and they dwelt with him all the time that David was in the stronghold.5 Now the prophet Gad said to David, "Do not stay in the stronghold; depart, and go to the land of Judah." So David departed and went into the forest of Hereth. (1 Samuel 22: 1– 5 NKJV).

The problems people face on their jobs - such as bully bosses, difficult colleagues, a heavy workload, threat to safety, verbal assaults, physical abuses - drain the most joy from their lives. The thing is that a difficult boss, as many people say, is "a task master." The classic bossy tasmaster is a bully, difficult in relationship, belittling, burned-out, controlling, insecure, micromanaging, namby-pamby, or paranoid. The real question is, what kind of shock absolver do you have to cushion the negative effects you face when you get to work? All these assaults on your person, abuses of your personality and belittling of your potential can cause one serious health crisis and even mental or psychological disorientation. If a deliberate effort is not made to have and maintain a balanced life in a hostile environment, one can begin to experience psychiatric problems.

According to Suzette Elgin, a **hostile environment can make you sick or kill you!** Elgin points out certain negative things that people pick up in a hostile environment.[1]

- Hostile language can kill one just as hostile driving can. Hostile language hurts and frustrates and confuses people. The damage it causes to people's heart and mind takes place slowly, over time, and is not readily visible resulting in rage and fits of anger.
- Exposure to chronic verbal abuse does leave one with obvious cuts and bruises which results in ulcers, migraine headaches, high blood pressure, allergy attacks, accidents in the home and

in the workplace and on the highway, colds, rashes, depression and every sort of misery.

- A hostile environment makes one an angry and cynical person. Angry and cynical people are five times as likely to die under 50 as people who are calm and trusting.[2]
- Another survey notes an association between social relationships and health. More socially isolated or less socially integrated people are less healthy, psychologically and physically, and more likely to die untimely from cardiac related problems.[3]

During the time of David's crisis, something stood out from his character: an ability to still bond with his family and minister to others in crisis. David was in serious crisis, yet he did not allow that to get into his way of family character and frustrated colleagues. Some other people would actually manifest transfer of aggression, become withdrawn, disorganized and wear a long face. David became succour for others. **In a hostile environment learn to knock off the things and people that upset you by becoming a city of refuge for others.** Learn to know and understand that when you are in a hostile environment, not everyone is hostile to you. Therefore, control your passion and emotions with a balance of life and uplift. Since water seeks its own level, in a hostile environment, it is only when you try to fulfill others, forget your pains and minister to others that you yourself can find succour and fulfillment. No matter how much life is hostile to you, there are two things that the hostile environment cannot take away from you. These are: family character and frustrated colleagues.

Strengthen your family character. David did not forget his constituency: his family. David knew that it was the only thing he had on earth that could not be taken away from him. In his hour of torment, chased by King Saul, he found time to be with his family. He did not just find time to stay with his family; he both cared for them and sought for their protection from harm. Forsaking your family in your hostile environment is a sure-fire path to your failure. You will burn out quickly if you do not maintain a healthy balance between your work and personal life. Be clear with yourself and emotions about your personal obligations, and do not let your hostile environment take precedence over your family life. "Strong and healthy family structures are essential for the human wellbeing,"[4] Says Koffi Annan

The United States Census Bureau defines a family as "two or more persons related by birth, marriage or adoption who reside in the same household." The emphasis however is on relationships within a biological or marital relationship. Of course, David's actions captures the richness of family life in — celebrating anniversaries, wiping runny noses, caring for an elderly parent, practicing spelling lessons, tucking in one's children to sleep, and kissing one's spouse goodnight. In contrast to the sometimes-hostile world of professional life, learning, business and career, one economist once observed, "The real world is the world around the kitchen table, the world of the nursery, the world of the bedroom." [5]

Claiming that family matters is not simply an appeal to sentiment, political philosophers, social historians, civic and religious leaders throughout the ages have praised the family as the foundation of the social order, the bedrock of a nation, and the bastion of civilization. Cicero, the notable Greek Philosopher, for example, spoke of the family as "the first society" and "the seedbed of the state." The Universal Declaration of Human Rights of the United Nations (UN) describes the family as "the natural and fundamental group unit of society." [6]

The family is a universal and irreplaceable community, rooted in human nature, which is the basis for all societies at all times. As the cradle of life and love for each new generation, the family is the primary source of personal identity, self-esteem, and support for everyone. It is also the first and foremost school of life, uniquely suited to teach person's integrity, character, morals, responsibility, service, and wisdom. As the UN Program for the International Year of the Family (1994) states, the family provides: *"the natural framework for the emotional, financial, and material support essential to the growth and development of its members, particularly infants and children. . . . The family remains a vital means of preserving and transmitting cultural values."* [7]

So many people go through life everyday facing terror, abuses, verbal assaults and other forms of trauma in the places where they work, live or learn. Due to this, some go through their days not knowing where they belong, not knowing where their place in life is. You always hear stories from people saying, "I do not feel like I belong in my job." "I feel like an outcast." "Everyone is liked but I am condemned." Such people have lost self esteem.

Self-esteem is a person's main belief about himself or herself. A person's self-esteem is based on his or her actions, both as how as well as what he or she does. Although self-esteem varies from time to time, the pattern usually leans toward a healthy or unhealthy view of self. With healthy self-esteem, a person is more likely to succeed in life. The best place to feed self-esteem is in the family. So, the best feeling in the world is being able to return to a place where you can call home. A place where you feel like you belong, a place where no one can hurt you, a place where you can learn something new each day from the ones who love you the most. By making the effort to communicate with the members of our family, we know that we are loved and respected and that we belong.

A family is not only a living unit, but is a network of relationships. Family relationships can be biological, adoptive, foster, step, and in-law. Although family members live together while children are young, families should continue to exist in kin relationships throughout life. Family relationships also do not depend primarily on financial or friendship considerations; it depends on love and inner connection.

What makes a person strong, healthy, and joyful and singing in a hostile environment is a loving family bond. There is no one set of qualities that can be said to make a person strong. Indeed, what strengthens one person may not support another. Person's identified as being strong tend, however, to have some qualities in common in their families. Strength comes when each person in your family needs you for fulfillment. There is every tendency to wear a long face, feel discouraged, become nasty and nagging because of transfer of aggression. Find time to strengthen your family character, for as you do, you in turn relieve yourself of tension.

Show your love to each family member. Let the members in your family know you love them for who they are, not for what he or she does. Make it a habit to show your love for your family members in at least two ways each day: caring and support. Supportive members express love in words and actions. Love is a verbal expression of positive feelings in very concrete terms. It is that moment of life when nothing else matters but the presence of the one whom you carry in your heart. So, an atmosphere of love is the environment to share that feeling. Find and use a word that seems to describe vividly who your lover is to you. This moment of love is what makes you unique because these are little things that matter most. Drop a well worded card into her hand bag as she goes to work without her knowledge,; write a short note and keep it in her soap can as you travel out of town. Write a letter to her using the official address without anything to betray you did it until he or she opens it.

Love goes with words of character praise and commendation. Speak to the man's sense of strength and achievement. Commend his courage, let him know how much his labour makes the house cared for and protected. Talk to the woman's sense of beauty. Treasure her eyelashes, give her a pat on the back as she walks through your space; hold your hands when you sit together in a place and even make your eyes a center of attraction and attention for one another. Give the children a hug and loving peck.

- **Make conscious effort to let each member of your family know that they are special.** List at least three good qualities of each family member and post them on your refrigerator. Add to these qualities from time to time. And it doesn't hurt to tell each other how wonderful they are. My Son Ashim is a darling when it comes to this. On my 39th birthday, while I was still asleep, my Son came into our room and pasted on my bed his hand made birthday cards. One of them read: "Daddy, I love you so much." When I read the words and remembered that he was just eight years old at that time, it made more meaning to me. He made a conscious effort to convey his feeling to me.
- **Praise each other.** Make positive comments about each other. It may not hurt to tell dad that you missed him or how good mom's cooking is. Notice the positive qualities in each other and try not to focus on the negative qualities of each person.

Buy a gift item when coming back home when the day has been rough. Gifts speak a lot about our passion and state of heart. A gift no matter how little says: "I love you, you have a place in my heart, and you are a treasure I love to adore." In buying the gift you take attention away from your pain and becoming involved rather in giving some else joy. Luxury is both the possession and use of costly and choice things for personal enjoyment. Gifts have their place in marriage. Nicon Noga Hilton Hotel has a sales motto which says "Come let's spoil you a little." Spoil your spouse a little with gifts. Let them be gifts that speak, make a statement, fill up your space and present you positively. Take her out if she enjoys it once in a while; go for a trip to Okomu Oil palm plantation, Yankari Games reserve, Odudu Resort, or even for just a drink in a quiet part of town. Sometimes help change your environment from what your home looks like.

Luxury differs from person to person and from marriage to marriage depending on your level of income. But luxury speaks volume of sacrifice.

Luxury addresses what your spouse values, what your spouse cherishes and what gives your spouse a lift. There are two MTN adverts that I love so much as they speak volume of love. In one of them, this woman corporate executive was mad with her husband for disorganizing her before going for work. To make amends with the wife, the man asked his Son to call up his mum with his cell phone. As the woman fumed over the phone, she was surprised to know it was her son. "Mummy, daddy says he is sorry. He promised to buy you dinner if you forgiven him" the Son said. The promise of dinner and the thoughtfulness of love is luxury some cannot just afford to their detriment. In another advert, this young man Jerry was miles away from home but called up his darling early morning to adore her and give her a gift. What did Jerry give to her: the gift of nature, even the beauty of the rising early morning sun. Luxury has a lot to do with thoughtfulness.

Listen to the members in your family. Just do not let it go in one ear and come out the other. When someone in your family shares something with you, give that person your undivided attention and listen carefully.

Have family times to play together. Have regular times for the family to have fun together, such as playing board or card games. Try to have as many family meals together as possible. Do not discuss problems or concerns during these times unless it is absolutely necessary. Play cards together, ludo, ayo, draft, scrabble, monopoly or whatever you can. Put on your tape and do a karaoke together: sing along, stage a dance competition between yourselves, just have fun. Take your family out for a stroll.

Encourage family bonding time. Look for activities with which the whole family can bond together and spend special moments together, where everyone can feel close, have a feeling of acceptance, and unconditional love from the people who mean the most in their lives. To foster bonding, adopt Family rituals and incorporate them into everyday life. Make ordinary events, such as eating together and bedtime, special. Members "share" rather than just "do" what life requires (routine).

Again, use humor as a way to relieve tension and bring members closer together. Laughter is one act of recreation that you do not pay for. It is the cheapest and most easily available drug. Scripture says "laughter makes the heart merry like a good medicine." You can survive in a marriage where there is laughter. Make yourself both laughable and an object of laughter. Laughter is an ability to make instinctive noise. It is also an effort to express amusement and make merry. It can also involve tickling and giggling someone. Laughter is a very effective ingredient in relieving tension in an already charged society. Ours is a militarized society where a little disagreement sparks off fighting and all forms of hostilities. Therefore, find time to douse the tension of the abuse of market women, the abuse of *danfo* drivers, the stress of bad roads and traffic jams.

Laughter is good medicine for the physical body. It has been found to reduce levels of certain stress hormones and boost the immune system. According to a study reported at the American Psychosomatic Society meeting, *"A large study shows that happy adults with heart disease are 20% more likely than equally ill, dour patients to stay alive for 11 years."* Also, *"Happy people might be less likely to churn out a torrent of stress hormones, such as cortisol,"* says cardiologist Jerome Fleg.[8] Humor and laughter are cornerstones of a healthy emotional life. They help you to boost your energy level, feel more relaxed, reduce anxiety and diffuse anger. According to Bernie Siegel, *"Laughter sustains a more positive mood and reduces the amount of time you spend in a state of irritation, anxiety, and depression."*[9]

Similarly, Paul E. McGhee, "agrees and states, *"The sense of humor is one of the powerful tools to make certain that the daily mood and emotional state supports good health. It maintains a healthy lifestyle in general."*[10] Again, *"People could actually extend their life spans with positive emotions,"* says Beverly Brummett.[11] When all is said and done, humor and laughter create emotional and physical relief while representing optimism and hope. Now that's a great wellness prescription for a happy and healthy life!

People laugh for two reasons: to release or to repress feelings. Laughing to repress feelings is unhealthy. Try to laugh for fun and relaxation! It's a great way to release stress! Tracy Gaudet explains that researchers have found that laughter helps your immune system fight invading viruses and cancers. It lowers blood levels of the stress hormone cortisol and can lower your blood pressure and decrease heart strain.[12]

Several studies[13] have found people who survived a heart attack could cut the risk of a second heart attack by 20 percent just by enjoying 30 minutes of comedy a day. Other research shows laughter helps the cardiovascular system by giving the heart and lungs an aerobic workout and can reduce stress by helping to relax muscles.

Hospitals have found that therapeutic humor stimulates the release of endorphins; the body's own pain relievers, and can decrease the average hospital stay by two days! According to Anne Asher, Laughter is now being studied for its medicinal qualities. It improves heart functioning, reduces stress levels, has the power to heal relationships and is great for mental outlook. Because of its many health benefits, laughter can indirectly help manage chronic pain and speed recovery from injury.[14] Remember, without love there is no healing. With Love, healing is foreseeable. Having a family can be a fulfilling and an exciting experience. Our family life is an important part of our life. How we treat each other and the respect we give each other will affect our relationship with that person and could affect how that person feels about him or her. Families grow and change over time, so it is important that we have the skills to remain close to each other, and be able to keep our family relationships happy and healthy.

Parent-child relationships within the household are now characterized by a greater degree of equality and respect for each other's autonomy than they were in the past.[15] The interaction between parents and children is more intimate; there is a greater recognition of the psychological needs of children and a greater willingness on the part of parents to satisfy them.[16] But there has also been a decline in terms of the time that parents and (young) children spend together — partly as a result of the fact that many married women continue to work — which sometimes leads to a conflict between what parents want and what they are able to do.[17] The father's role within the household is also changing.[18] Parent-child relationships have become less hierarchical and authoritarian; a shift has occurred from households based on 'authority' to ones based on 'negotiation'.[19] Parent-child relationships are becoming increasingly characterized by freedom of choice and are therefore acquiring their own unique content.[20]

Strengthen your frustrated colleagues. One aspect of our humanity which we have problem with is the inability to lose focus of ourselves in troublesome times to seek the good and welfare of others. This is because every human being by nature is selfish. David shows us that becoming a city of refuge will give you both fulfillment and goodwill. It is only when you seek to fulfill others that you are fulfilled yourself; it is only when you seek to heal others that you are healed yourself. Let us consider the attitude of David. Those who were in distress, debt, and discontented gathered around him and he became their captain.

Those in distress (mâtsôq) means persons confined to a narrow place, filled with anguish and pain; then those in debt (nâshâ') means persons in financial pains, carrying burdens of interest payments, and those discontented (mar mârâh): persons whose lives were filled with bitterness, anger and heaviness.[21] That David became their captain meant that he became a head person in the sense of giving meaning and direction to their lives. The term captain also means that David became a governor of actions and ruler of lives. This is exactly what makes lives exciting. Some people who have pains would have to add the pains of others to their pains so that hope can spread round like a good perfume. In a hostile environment, you can be a reason for others to live and they will be eternally grateful that they meet someone like you.

Any observer of human emotions recognizes that certain circumstances and actions by others do indeed make us mad. When we are intentionally hurt, insulted, cheated, deceived, or made fun of--all these things arouse frustration, anger and aggression making people distrustful. Some theorists believe that anger just naturally results from frustration. This is called the frustration-aggression hypothesis.[22]

Our frustration will be more intense if our goal is highly desirable, if we "get close" to our goal and expect to get it, if the barrier to our goal unexpectedly appears and seems unjustified or unfair, and if we "take things personally."[23] In a hostile environment there are several physiological reactions that accompany frustration, including higher blood pressure, sweating, and greater energy. Some other psychosomatic symptoms also occur. Heart diseases occur more often in people who are cynics and distrustful but hold onto their anger. Some of us explode, others swallow feelings. Our blood pressure sometimes goes up more when we explode. At other times it goes up more when we swallow the feelings, depending on the situation. The more physiologically damaging anger reactions seem to occur under two extreme conditions, namely, when we feel utterly helpless, or, the opposite, when we have overly optimistic expectations of reaching unreachable goals.[24]

One reason many people do not achieve their goals is that they do not know how to handle frustration. By contrast, people who are successful in any field have handled much frustration as they achieve their success. In today's world of conveniences, learning to deal with frustrations can be very challenging. However, it is something that you can help someone both to learn and to do.

The first thing to do to strengthen your frustrated colleagues is awareness. Help them to realize and accept that there will be frustrations and that we would love to plow our way through them to get where we want to go. By so doing, we can even learn to enjoy the process.

The second thing to do to strengthen your frustrated colleagues is to help them look at the little--and big—failures in their lives as feedback. Let them see the frustrating elements of the boss as opportunities for learning what does *not* work and what does work in a place. Then, let them think of a better way to do it, and the next chance they have, try it out. Frustration is caused by not accomplishing or getting what you want within an environment. Teach them that instead of dwelling on failures or frustrations, they should focus on what can achieve and then build on your successes. Start by selecting only one or two things to work on at a time. Try to accomplish small goals initially. Once you can handle small goals, move on to larger ones. Every night before going to sleep, teach them to check their day: Where did I gain and where did I lose?

The third thing to do for frustrated colleagues is to have a supportive attitude. Be packed with motivational capsules each day of the week as you go to work. Let courage be found on your lips, wear a smile in the heat of queries, help them sing when termination stares them in the face, but above all, give the word that would carry them on. Here is a very good example: "You have to put more into life than you take out of it. Destruction lurks around where destiny beckons. Never say never, when you have not seen the end of the road." Many people who constantly experience frustration probably have the opposite attitude.[25]

- Quitters never win, and winners never quit. Losing your control means you're a quitter.
- When you quit because of frustration, you lose credibility and self-confidence. Adopt the motto: "I will overcome frustration."
- The best way of dealing with frustration is to accept it as a challenge -- and love it.
- Focus on your progress and take pleasure every step of the way -- even if it's only a small amount.
- Frustration is called idol worship -- because we're taking marching orders from the wrong boss.
- Life is difficult and the path to greatness is paved with frustration. You can't get to heaven on roller skates.
- When we know that God provides the challenge, then we know we can succeed.

Help lower their expectations and reduce their frustrations. **Think of it this way...**When people learn to walk, they fall down. It's expected. If they would not, they would never learn how to walk independently. When we fall down, that little failure (and sometimes those falls can be nasty) is what teaches us what *not* to do. Then, as you walk more and more, you figure out what *yet* to do. You are learning from your mistakes. You begin to understand how to coordinate leg and arm movements with your sense of balance and with what your eyes and ears perceive. True, the process takes time and effort, but it becomes more and more automatic the more you practice. Unquestionably, it is very worthwhile. Then, before you know it...you are walking! [26]

Four, help your frustrated colleagues to relax at work and not worry about the worry that yet does not worry them. Relax. I realize that this is more easily said than done, especially if the persons are feeling embarrassed or angry. Remember that all the other workers in the other places have had to cope with their own bad bosses' or colleagues' insults or threats. Therefore, help them to come to see the harassment as an indirect confirmation of potentiality than as criticism. Help them take a deep breath.

Five, help them take control of their lives. They should remember that frustration is a sign that one is feeling out of control. If you show your bad boss or colleagues that you have control of the situation, it will be easier for him to calm down. Often the best way to do this is to focus on your harasser to do him good. It need not be far away. If you are in the office, for example, just move yourself away from the place he or she is demanding your reputation, because they do so to theirs in return. In other words, *make you no let people see am finish*. Protect the bad boss-harasser from harassing himself or herself. In enabling your frustrated colleagues to take control of their lives, teach them not to yell at themselves, curse themselves, and abuse their bad boss or colleagues. That will only make things worse for both of them. Teach them to try to ignore the harasser without ignoring their work. I know this sounds confusing. Keep in mind that your goal is to have your work, feel more in control so that his tantrum is no longer necessary. Begin by acknowledging how upset your bad boss is and try to put a smile in his anger.

Similarly, in taking control of their lives strengthen them not to give in to the hostile environment. The worst thing you can do is to give your bad boss or bad colleague a sign for something he's throwing frustrating elements at you for. Bad bosses or dangerous colleagues are smart. If you give in, they quickly learn that throwing hostility is an effective way of getting the things they want. **Never quit out of frustration.** "Quitting" is another form of giving in to frustration. Appreciate that this is a tough world and we have to be persistent in order to accomplish. Never turn back in midstream. Follow it through to the end. Let your frustrated colleagues consider how many projects they began -- and then gave up -- because they became frustrated and lost patience. Help them Make a list of things they started and quit because they seemed too difficult. Now let them calculate the disappointment and loss they suffered by not accepting the frustration. How do they repair this fault? Again, let them look at the list of things they have quitted. Help them choose this one hostile environment and resolve to see it through. And for the rest of their lives, once they undertake something, resolve never to quit. (Unless you are objectively sure that it's "not worth it" -- i.e. you initially misjudged the amount of effort required relative to the final payoff.)

Six, help your frustrated colleagues to offer their bad bosses more appropriate choices. This will help them regain a feeling of power and control over their lives. Let them allow their bosses choose what manner of way to approach their work, what deadlines they can conveniently meet and what moods they can easily adjust to. Teach them to offer these choices in a calm, matter-of-fact manner, so they do not come across as bribes for stopping the harassment. Otherwise, their harasser would probably throw more frustrating elements at them so that he or she can be bribed again. Change takes time because your mind is very good at keeping you where you are. It is almost impossible to change over night, so there is no need to get frustrated. Just acknowledge that it will take time to change your present limitations and take it one step at a time. As you gain more control over yourself and improve, you will become less frustrated and more confident in your ability to eventually succeed.

Seven, listen to your frustrated colleagues. Research has shown that attentive listening is actually good for our health. When we are really listening, our blood pressure goes down, our heartbeat moderates and our body shows the healthful changes associated with relaxation. When our language behavior makes other people enjoy being around us and look forward to talking with us, when we clean up our language environment so that verbal strength is part of our life, we do more for our health and well-being than we could ever accomplish in any other way. If for no other reason, and no matter what your gender, that's why you should bother to focus on others in your hostile environment. A change of focus for survival can result from lack of development of one's spiritual senses.

CHAPTER ELEVEN:

DEVELOP YOUR SPIRITUAL SENSES

Then they told David, saying, "Look, the Philistines are fighting against Keilah, and they are robbing the threshing floors."2 Therefore David inquired of the LORD, saying, "Shall I go and attack these Philistines?" And the LORD said to David, "Go and attack the Philistines, and save Keilah."3 But David's men said to him, "Look, we are afraid here in Judah. How much more then if we go to Keilah against the armies of the Philistines?"4 Then David inquired of the LORD once again. And the LORD answered him and said, "Arise, go down to Keilah. For I will deliver the Philistines into your hand."5 And David and his men went to Keilah and fought with the Philistines, struck them with a mighty blow, and took away their livestock. So David saved the inhabitants of Keilah.6 Now it happened, when Abiathar the son of Ahimelech fled to David at Keilah, that he went down with an ephod in his hand.7 ¶ And Saul was told that David had gone to Keilah. So Saul said, "God has delivered him into my hand, for he has shut himself in by entering a town that has gates and bars."8 Then Saul called all the people together for war, to go down to Keilah to besiege David and his men.9 When David knew that Saul plotted evil against him, he said to Abiathar the priest, "Bring the ephod here."10 Then David said, "O LORD God of Israel, Your servant has certainly heard that Saul seeks to come to Keilah to destroy the city for my sake.11 "Will the men of Keilah deliver me into his hand? Will Saul come down, as Your servant has heard? O LORD God of Israel, I pray, tell Your servant." And the LORD said, "He will come down."12 Then David said, "Will the men of Keilah deliver me and my men into the hand of Saul?" And the LORD said, "They will deliver you."13 So David and his men, about six hundred, arose and departed from Keilah and went wherever they could go. Then it was told Saul that David had escaped from Keilah; so he halted the expedition. And David stayed in strongholds in the wilderness, and remained in the mountains in the Wilderness of Ziph. Saul sought him every day, but God did not deliver him into his hand. (1 Samuel 23: 1– N KJV).

A hostile environment is mind-draining as well as energy-sapping. It fills one with horrible images and threatening circumstances. In an atmosphere of unexpected attacks and injustice we are bound to make several mistakes both in reactions and relationships except we develop our spiritual side and allow it to rule and direct our activities. David shows us the extreme importance of spiritual development in a hostile environment for winning the battle of wits and mind.

Because David knew his passion and purpose as a shepherd, when Keilah a city of Judah was under attack from the Philistines, he inquired of the Lord if he should go, and the Lord gave him permission to go deliver the city. Having delivered the city, now a hero and champion, he heard that Saul was coming to Keilah to attack him. Again he inquired of the Lord if he should stay and if the inhabitants of the city would deliver him to Saul. The Lord asked him to leave the city, for Saul would not only come but the inhabitants of the city would deliver him to Saul.

The term "inquire" (shâ'al shâ'êl) means to ask counsel, or to consult for expert advice. One serious aspect of this consultation and request is the ability to hear the Lord clearly and listen to the counsel He offers. This is because, God is Spirit and an understanding of the ways He speaks and getting to know them would play a crucial part for our survival in a hostile environment. In other words, to **survive in a hostile environment, develop your spiritual senses**. There are two basic parts of our humanity; these are the spiritual and physical components. The physical components of our lives are made up of the things we see, smell, hear, feel and touch. Our ability to effectively relate to and with any or all of these defines our humanity. However, we must also note that these physical realities also have a spiritual side. Our ability to hear, see, feel, smell and touch the supernatural would determine every step we take in the battle for survival in a hostile environment.

Some people are in greater business mess, career disaster and administrative strangulation because they never consulted with the Lord before they took some steps in the hostile environment. We must know that the human heart is desperately wicked and none can know it except the Lord. There are persons we have favoured, thinking in our times of trial they will do the same for us in return. There are persons whose errors we have helped to cover up thinking that in our times of crisis they will speak up for us. We have put food on the table of some of these persons, we have materially empowered them to succeed, and we have administratively orchestrated their rapid rise in management and even personally supervised and launched their growth in our various institutions and establishments. Do not be foolish enough to think that in your hour of need and crisis, even where you have been a super hero that they will stand up for you. A hostile environment is like life in the jungle. In the jungle, it is everyone for himself or herself and God for us all. Be like David, develop your spiritual senses.

Pathways to develop our spiritual senses. Our spiritual sense is a great determinant of survival in the hostile environment. David therefore consulted with or asked the Lord for direction at a time when the only trusted friend was the Lord. There are basically two things to note in this process of spiritual development or consultation. When David asked the Lord for counsel, there was no definite pattern in focus through which God spoke, yet David knew it was the Lord. When Abiathar the priest brought the ephod; David consulted with the Lord through it and also knew it was the Lord that spoke. The ephod was a leather-like bag in which the Urim and thumim were placed. These were like dice through which the priest could interpret the mind of God on a matter. The most important thing in all of these was the willingness of David to seek spiritual direction by hearing what God had to say on the matter.

God is interested in your welfare and well being and can speak concerning your hostile environment. There are actions that can only lead you into greater pains and regrets. Find time to listen. God speaks in many ways, many times throughout our days. In our trials, the Lord may send a comforting word through a friend. During that special time of need, God may use that friend to plant a seed. A tiny seed sown just for that trial can cause your heart to smile. God may send a friend to impart words of wisdom into your heart. God can even speak in the night, even when there is no one in sight. God will use the events of life to draw you closer to Himself. For God is still quite an active friend, speaking to the hearts of all men. Listening to God is an important part of the Christian life. God desires to speak to us and we have the privilege of listening to His instruction and guidance.

So, how can we discipline ourselves to hear the voice of God? Consider these practical tips: Plan ahead. Restructure your schedule so you can spend uninterrupted time with your Heavenly Father. Find a quiet place and bring along your Bible, notebook, and pen. Perhaps you enjoy worshipping with music and would like to bring along your favorite worship music. Prepare yourself mentally, emotionally, and physically. It is essential that we come to God with a pure heart, righteous motives, and a desire to hear from Him. Spend time confessing sin and receiving God's forgiveness. Spend time in prayer, worship, Bible reading, and meditation on God's Word. As you read God's Word, ask Him to speak to you. God often speaks to His children through His written Word. Wait expectantly. This is not a time to zoom out or think of the activities for later in the day. If something apart from God's voice comes to your mind, jot it down. This will free your mind to be able to concentrate on God and listen for His instruction. Spend time in silence, waiting for God to speak in your spirit. Feel free to ask Him questions and then await His answer. Some people like to write down what they hear from God or any direction they receive about a certain issue. Obey whatever God tells you to do. Continue your time of waiting on God throughout the day. Always be listening for His voice.

People often wonder if they can hear God's voice, and how to determine whether it is God's voice or their own. God speaks to us in many ways. Sometimes it is through a voice that we can hear. Sometimes it is through peace that flows over our heart. Sometimes it is through another person. Sometimes it is through a new insight that suddenly comes into our mind and seems to solve a problem that has been keeping us confused. "Call upon me and I will answer you and show you great and mighty things..." (Jeremiah 33:3). God wants us to call out in faith, and if we keep ourselves open, we will receive an answer. It will not always be the answer we want, and it may not always seem at first to solve our problem, but in time we will know that it was God and that it was the answer we needed to hear. Do not be afraid to trust that God does answer us. When we are open to the presence of God in all the moments and through all the pressures of our lives, we will find that we feel God's presence, and hear God's voice. It is always the case that when we hear God's voice, our soul grows more deeply in the love of God. And, the more deeply we love God, the more aware of God's voice we become.

So how can we know whether we are hearing the voice of God? The Bible gives us basic keys or filters through which every possible leading should be judged. We are to carefully examine the thoughts and intentions of our hearts -- and the words of godly people who may have influence on us by their words and actions -- through the use of these seven keys:

God speaks through Scripture: *"All Scripture is given by inspiration of God, and is profitable for doctrine, for reproof, for correction, for instruction in righteousness, that the man of God may be complete, thoroughly equipped for every good work."* (II Timothy 3:16-17). The timeless wisdom of God's word

106

has personally touched each of us. We have all felt at one time or another that the passage we were reading at a moment of need was meant especially for us. This is one of the mystical facts that make the Bible unique.

- Write down the passage of scripture dropped into your spirit man.
- Meditate on the passage and immerse yourself in its meaning to see what God is revealing about himself, purpose and plans.
- Identify the specific things the Lord is asking you to do through the passage. Such as adjustments and commitments to improve your life and job.
- Watch to see how God by Himself will use that scripture throughout that day.

God speaks through The Holy Spirit speaking to our heart: *"For this is the covenant that I will make with the house of Israel after those days, says the Lord: I will put my laws into their minds, and I will write them on their hearts and I will be their God, and they shall be my people. And they shall not teach everyone his fellow citizen, and everyone his brother, saying, 'know the Lord,' for all will know Me, from the least to the greatest of them"* (Hebrews 8:10-11). Not a sound but a voice! A voice can shake you to your very soul because a voice is not necessarily heard with the ears.

- A voice is heard in your mind or your heart, not a sound.
- The voice gives you peace and not torment. **God speaks through the peace in our hearts:** "Let the peace of Christ rule in your hearts, to which indeed you were called in one body; and be thankful" (Colossians 3:15).
- The message that comes from the voice is non-coercive but suggestive and persuasive.
- The message of the voice involves a God-sized assignment.

In March 2005, I was in Kano, Nigeria ministering when a member of the organizing committee for Baptist Day Rally of Edo Baptist Conference called to inform me that I had been chosen to minister in the meeting. When I thought it through, I called back that I would not accept the invitation because of personal reasons. The chairman of the committee on getting the information called me that I should reconsider my decision, which I refused to do. We spoke for forty five minutes on phone and I refused to be persuaded to change my mind. As I dropped the phone, I heard a voice that said "Well done my boy. Call him back that you will minister." I raised all my arguments which informed my decision. The voice said "remember, the politics of relationship. If you do not accept this assignment, you would add your friends to your enemies." I immediately called the chairman that I would accept the invitation. I was glad I did because it was a ministration I will never forget for the unction to minister to the political and spiritual powers of the state gathered in that meeting.

God speaks through a word of knowledge, a word of wisdom, prophecy, dreams and visions too. Dreams and visions are a regular part of our lives. Daydreams and visions are sparked many times by our being at a certain place at a certain time. "When they heard the king, they departed; and behold, the star which they had seen in the East went before them, till it came and stood over where the young Child was. When they saw the star, they rejoiced with exceedingly great joy. And when they had come into the house, they saw the young Child with Mary His mother, and fell down and worshiped Him. And when they had opened their treasures, they presented gifts to Him: gold, frankincense, and myrrh. Then, being divinely warned in a dream that they should not return to Herod, they departed for their own country another way. Now when they had departed, behold, an angel of the Lord appeared to Joseph in a dream, saying, "Arise, take the young Child and His mother, flee to Egypt, and stay there until I bring you word; for Herod will seek the young Child to destroy Him. "When he arose, he took the young Child and His mother by night and departed for Egypt, and was there until the death of Herod that it might be fulfilled which was spoken by the Lord through the prophet, saying, "Out of Egypt I called My Son." (Matthew 2: 9 – 15 NKJV).

- The message is always unique to you as an individual.
- The vision addresses you case specifically and leaves a tangible meaning on it.
- The vision is free of clouds and confusion and points you toward grace.

God speaks through others for Godly counsel: God speaks to us through people. You have to be cautious here too; but if God can speak through a donkey, He can speak through other people to us. God will speak through your children, the person you intend to marry, your spouse, close friends, small groups, and the church. This is why God gave us spiritual leaders, pastors, shepherds, and elders. You should not walk into a worship service and not have God speak to you through someone. You should ask Him to speak; and every time you ask Him to He will. **God will speak into your life through people in ways you will not even get from (although it will agree with) the Bible.** *"Where there is no counsel, the people fall: but in the multitude of counselors there is safety"* (Proverbs 11:14). *"By the mouth of two or three witnesses every fact may be confirmed."* (Matthew 18:16).

God speaks through Circumstances/Timing: This is exactly where as human beings we have a problem because God will use any circumstance to work out his purpose. There is a divine agenda for every life, therefore let us watch out in our difficult moments and hostile environment to see how God is at work to perform his purpose. Even when things are wrong, the harassments are terrible, the threats are intimidating and verbal assaults increase, ask God what he wants you to know and see in the matter.

"After these things he (Paul) left Athens and went to Corinth. And he found a certain Jew named Aquila, a native of Pontus, having recently come from Italy with his wife Priscilla, because Claudius had commanded all the Jews to leave Rome. He came to them, and because he was of the same trade, he stayed with them and they were working; for by trade they were tent-makers" (Acts 18:1-3) This relationship between Paul, Aquila and Priscilla happened as a result of circumstances, yet it has become one of the most important strategic partnerships in the book of Acts. Simply put, when a hunch "works out right", it makes an impression. We do not know that a chain of events has any significance until we recall and review that they are connected in a way that ultimately leads us in a certain direction. These events do not accidentally happen. They give you the strength to continue to follow the clues that God has given you for the direction He wants you to go. We are in the process of making an important, life-changing decision that would affect us to survive the harassments in our hostile environment.

- In our circumstances of hostility as we seek for divine counsel watch out for what appear to be spiritual markers in your life. A spiritual marker identifies a time of transition, decision, or direction when you clearly knew that God had guided you in the past almost along the same line.[1]
- Take a spiritual inventory of your life to times and periods when you faced crisis and see how and what God led you to do. These might have

to do with you family background, origin of the job or career, marital question, relationship problems, etc.

Profits for developing our spiritual senses. David and his men were ale to escape from Saul so that Saul gave up the pursuit. Saul would have felt undone and disgraced after the people of Keilah gave him every assurance that David would be caught, more so, the city had two gates and walls. The term "escape" (mâlat-Hebrew) means to rescue a thing. It describes a situation where something catches you to hurt you, but you slip away from the person's grip. The Lord knows the beginning from the end; therefore, as the omniscient one, who knows, sees and understands all things, His counsel can help you slip away from danger. There are queries that have been carefully and systematically constructed to nail you. When the Lord teaches and shows you what to answer, you dismiss all its negative efforts as a mere rhetoric.

One of the greatest benefits of our salvation has to be that of hearing God speak to us personally. There can be no intimate relationship with our heavenly Father without it. But, as easy as it is for us to speak to Him, the average Christian has a hard time hearing His voice. This is not the way the Lord intended it to be. Learning to clearly distinguish God's voice is invaluable. Instead of going through life blindly, we can have the wisdom of God guide and protect us. **There is not a single person today who will not have their life radically transformed by hearing the voice of the Lord better.** The worst marital problem is one word from the Lord away from a total turn-around. If you have a sickness or disease, one living word from the Lord will instantly heal you. If you are in financial crisis, the Lord knows exactly how to turn your situation around. It's just a matter of hearing His voice. The Lord constantly speaks to us and gives us His direction. It's never the Lord who is not speaking, but it's us who are not hearing.

A number of years ago I was going through a tough time in my life in which I really needed to hear the voice of God on a constant basis to keep me moving forward through the obstacles that I was facing in ministry. I found that the hardest time to hear the voice of God is when seemingly negative circumstances are screaming in your ears and glaring in your eyes. But I also knew that this "crisis" had given me an opportunity to press into hearing and seeing Him like never before. Circumstances that are challenging can either be a brick wall to keep you from moving up to a higher level of hearing, or with the help of the Spirit it can become a doorway into greater intimacy with God.

During difficult times, find it necessary to focus intently on Jesus and to immerse yourself in the truth of His Word. These times usually begin with a period of pressing through your own fears, thoughts, doubts and confusion. You often find yourself praying through the Psalms of David because so many of them begin in fear and doubt but end in hope and faith. During this season, when darkness seems to be closing in around you like black turbulent waters, each day at work, school or in that hostile environment, journey through your fears and doubts in order to find those "still waters" where the voice of God can be heard and His loving embrace felt. When you develop your spiritual sense you would reach into the darkness and find the hand of your faithful Father who would lovingly lead you through the pain and the fears right into His peaceful arms. By the end of the hostile journey you would have heard the voice of your Shepherd speak words of peace into your storm.

The journey of learning to hear the voice of God in trying times imparts perseverance and tenacity within you. It wells up faith within you in the supernatural and makes you grow tough in tough times. These times also give birth to testimonies of God's faithfulness that would carry you like a lifeboat through many more storms. Usually in the beginning of our Christian journey of walking with God, we rely on the stories of others to give us the faith to face the storms but as our journeys take us through these storms, they become personal testimonies of His faithfulness that give to us greater faith and also give faith to those whose journeys have just begun. You become a source of hope and inspiration to others, a scripture that they can point to, a walking miracle in the streets, in fact a seed for those who are down trodden.

Take a few moments each day to sit in a quiet place. Close your eyes and try to feel God's presence around you. Take some time to tell God what is in your heart. Speak to God like you would to your most intimate friend. After you have said all you need to say, sit in stillness again, and let God speak to you. You might feel a warmth, you might suddenly have a thought that had not occurred to you before, you might immediately have a fresh understanding of something that has been confusing you, you might have a clarity about an action you should take, or you might notice a gentle and serene peace all around you. Let the presence of God move around your soul as you sit quietly. When you feel God's silence again, you will know that it is time to end your prayer and thank God for being so present with you.

- You must ask Him to speak; to speak to you personally; and you must actively seek His will. The same way your spouse will say "Let's talk", or "Talk to me" – you must say to the Lord: "Talk to me". People say the want the will of God; but the will of God is something you must actively seek.

- You must expect Him to speak; and you in turn listen! Here is where you do an analysis of your life schedule: do you have any listening time for God? Is there any time set aside in your life for your relationship with God?

- We must prepare ourselves to hear and recognize God's voice. To accurately hear and recognize God's voice, all known sin must be acknowledged, confessed and forgiven. Sin in our lives causes interruption of our communication line to Heaven because the essence of sin is self dislocation. Prayer is the opposite of self-will, it is God's-will. It is difficult for God to break through our strong wall of self-will.

Problems with developing our spiritual senses. God desires to speak to every one of us living, learning or working in a hostile environment. He desires to reveal His will to us, and to be actively involved in leading us. This has always been the desire of God. From the beginning of the creation of humanity, and continuing throughout history, God has wanted to communicate with His creation. He walked in the cool of the day with Adam. This desire on God's part to reveal His word to us is often not understood by Christians because we do not understand the full meaning of what he says or we do not hear him at all. God intends for there to be a living dependency on our hearing Him speak by His Spirit. If we miss that and simply rely on research and knowledge, we will fail to come to the place of truly being led by the Spirit. We will end up walking in what we think, or what some people think.

Poor relationship: The major key to knowing His voice is developing an intimate relationship with Him. There is no substitute! Our number one priority is to keep us in a position to hear from God. He wants to lead us and guide us. He is not holding back. We take ourselves out of the position to hear from God. **We must be born again** - The first requirement is to <u>know Him</u> personally, because Jesus said "My sheep hear voice..." John10: 3,4.

Poor listening: How many of us think that we are good listeners? Women tend to be better listeners than men. Husbands are notorious for being poor listeners. We are all familiar with the scene of a husband reading the newspaper while his wife is trying to talk. His response is "Yes, dear. Uhuh. Mmmm. Is that so?" But we all know he is not really listening. Suddenly if she pulls down the paper and says, "Have you heard what I said?!!" The man does not know what to reply because he actually never heard anything, though he was there. Two men were talking one day. One of them said, "My wife talks to herself a lot." His friend answered, "Mine does, too, but she does not know it. She thinks I am listening." But poor listening is not just attributed to men. All of us sometimes listen poorly — like when we are on airplanes and the stewardess is making the required safety announcement.

President Franklin D. Roosevelt got tired of smiling that big smile and saying the usual things at all those White House receptions. So, one evening he decided to find out whether anybody was paying attention to what he was saying. As each person came up to him with extended hand, he flashed that big smile and said, "I murdered my grandmother this morning." People would automatically respond with comments such as "How lovely!" or "Just continue with your great work!" Nobody listened to what he was saying, except one foreign diplomat. When the president said, "I murdered my grandmother this morning," the diplomat responded softly, "I'm sure she had it coming to her." People often do not really hear what is said.[2]

Poor receivers: Radio and television stations transmit twenty-four hours a day, seven days a week; but we only hear them when we turn the receiver on and tune it in. Failure to hear the signal doesn't mean the station isn't transmitting. Likewise, God is constantly transmitting His voice to His sheep, but few are turned on and tuned in. Most Christians are busy pleading with God in prayer to transmit when the problem is with their receivers. The first thing we need to do is fix our receivers, believe that God is already speaking and start listening. However, that takes time, effort, and focus. **The average Christian's lifestyle is so busy; it is not conducive to hearing God's voice.** For instance, what is your typical answer to the question, "How are you?" Many of you probably answer something about being very busy. I often say, "I'm busier than a one-arm paper hanger." All of us seem to be busier than ever, and that's one of the BIG reasons we don't hear the voice of the Lord better. We're just too busy.

Jesus would usually say after uttering a parable, "He who has ears to hear, let him hear." It is possible to hear with our physical ears and not hear with our ears of understanding. We've all experienced this in many ways. But ears to hear are what we need to understand the spiritual truth

113

necessary to live our lives. Not everyone has ears to hear. Our ears can become clogged by the wax of worldliness so that we fail to hear what the Spirit is trying to communicate.

Many voices: There are actually four types of "voices" which we hear speaking to us, and it is important that we learn to distinguish each one so that we are able to discern the true voice of God. The voice that is perhaps the most obvious is our own voice. In addition to our speaking voice, we also talk to ourselves inside our heads, we see images and pictures inside our heads, we have emotions and feelings and desires, and so on. Our minds tell us what we think, our wills tell us what we want, and our emotions tell us how we feel. The Bible refers to our minds, wills, and emotions as our "flesh nature."

Another type of voice which clamours for our attention is the "voice" of other people. Sometimes people say things which are true, noble, and good, and sometimes people say things which are just the opposite. This book will provide some guidance to help you discern what you are hearing from the "voice" of other people.

The third type of voice is the "voice" of the devil. The devil has crafty ways of speaking to us which he has perfected over the millennia. He does not appear before us in a red, cloven-hoofed suit and speak out loud to us; he is much more subtle than that. What he does is to throw thoughts into our minds like flaming arrows, and he speaks to us through the worldly ideas and viewpoints that he has injected into other people. By the time you finish this book you will have a better understanding of how to "extinguish all the flaming arrows of the evil one" (Ephesians 6:16). The fourth voice is the voice of God.

Lack of discernment: The most difficult part of hearing God is the fact that it takes time to learn to discern God's voice. Jesus tells us in John 10:4b and 5, *"...and the sheep follow Him, for they know His voice. Yet they will by no means follow a stranger, but will flee from him, for they do not know the voice of strangers."* It is by practicing, by reason of use, that we are able to discern whether what we hear is of God, our flesh, or the Devil.

The supermarket mentality: I usually hear people say or pray "Lord, I am going to do this thing, if it is not your will, stop me from doing it if I am wrong, but bless it if I am right." This is the problem with hurry, busyness and sign seeking. It is based on experience, on a head factor of reasoning only. This is what most people do because it is an easy thing so that when they make a mistake they take a swipe on God.

God does not speak to us in our minds; He speaks to us in our spirits because that is where the Holy Spirit lives. Unfortunately, we tend to spend most of our thought life in our heads, in other words in "the mind of the flesh" focused on the sensory world around us where our physical senses and our thoughts, feelings, desires, and emotions are constantly being bombarded and stimulated in worldly, carnal, fleshly ways. We tend to live on the shallow surface, rarely venturing deeper where the Spirit of God lives within us. The result is that many of us do not know where our spirits are, nor how to hear and be led by our spirits. Because of this we leave ourselves wide open to fall for the many deceptions of the devil.

How do you know God is speaking to you? The following tests will help you determine if God is speaking to you.

The first test is the confirmation of God's written Word - the Bible. Everything that God says will agree with His written Word. He will never tell you to sin or go against a teaching in His Word. This simple test can clarify many "messages." We must, however, be careful not to read the written Word with any preconceived ideas of what it is saying.

The second test is the confirmation of godly counsel. God has placed people in our lives to help us to hear His voice. These people may include pastors, teachers, parents, and godly friends. In most cases, they will confirm the voice of God to you and help you to see His plan. This is not to say that you should rely on them solely. These people are human and can have their own feelings and fears distort their objectivity. However, they can be a very valuable source of confirmation when you are uncertain of God's voice.

The third test is the confirmation through circumstances. Christians can carefully study their situation for indications of God's will. Some Christians have called this the Gideon method or "putting out the fleece." When God told Gideon that he was to lead Israel into battle against their enemies, Gideon put a fleece out on the ground in order to receive a sign that God was really speaking to him. If you feel led to use this test, come to God with a humble attitude and not a spirit of testing Him. Pray for God to reveal His will and carefully watch the circumstances that relate to that decision.

If you feel that God is speaking a message to you but you are not really sure if it is from God here are some good questions to ask your self about the message.

1. Does it line up with the Holy Bible, the written scriptures?

2. Does it lead you into a closer relationship with God, a greater unity with Him?
3. Does it lead you into expressing love, which is putting God's benefit and the benefit of others before your own benefit?
4. Does it lead to a dying of yourself and a greater manifestation of Christ life in you?
5. Does it cause greater humility in you, and a greater dependence upon God?
6. Does it cause greater love, joy, and peace from God in you?

There is nothing you can achieve outside of God. So, winners discover the God factor in their life. God's plans for you are more extraordinary than anything you can imagine for yourself. Amazing things will happen as you learn to recognize God's signposts in your life, put your feet on His path, and commit yourself to follow where He leads. Your calling can only succeed if God is there to back you up. When you dream the dreams God has created you to pursue, He also equips you to fulfill them. Your life's mission and meaning doesn't "just happen" without your participation. Partnering with God to live your calling requires making decisions. Learning to make good decisions about life choices is an essential part of spiritual maturity.

CHAPTER TWELVE:

DO NOT LAY HANDS ON THE ANOINTED.

Now it happened, when Saul had returned from following the Philistines, that it was told him, saying, "Take note! David is in the Wilderness of En Gedi."2 Then Saul took three thousand chosen men from all Israel, and went to seek David and his men on the Rocks of the Wild Goats.3 So he came to the sheepfolds by the road, where there was a cave; and Saul went in to attend to his needs. (David and his men were staying in the recesses of the cave.)4 Then the men of David said to him, "This is the day of which the LORD said to you, 'Behold, I will deliver your enemy into your hand, that you may do to him as it seems good to you.'" And David arose and secretly cut off a corner of Saul's robe. 5 Now it happened afterward that David's heart troubled him because he had cut Saul's robe.6 And he said to his men, "The LORD forbid that I should do this thing to my master, the LORD'S anointed, to stretch out my hand against him, seeing he is the anointed of the LORD."7 So David restrained his servants with these words, and did not allow them to rise against Saul. And Saul got up from the cave and went on his way. (1 Samuel 24: 1– 7 NKJV).

It can be hell on earth if you do end up with a brutal boss or in an environment of sheer frustration with person (or persons) who is either capable of making you wish that you have never been born or a person you would really love to kill and walk away a free person (literally). According to Hornstein, author of *Brutal Bosses*, there are eight daily sins of a brutal boss which by extension do manifest in a hostile environment:[1]

- **Deceit:** Lying; giving false or misleading information through acts of omission or commission to make life difficult and troublesome.
- **Constraint:** Restricting subordinates' activities in domains outside of work, e.g., where they live, the people with whom they live, friendships, and civic activity. It is more or less a policed environment filled with suspense and spying.
- **Coercion:** threatening, excessive or inappropriate harm for noncompliance with a boss's or colleague's wishes especially where they have to do with undue favour.

- **Selfishness:** protecting themselves by blaming subordinates and making them the scapegoats for any problems that occur.
- **Inequity:** Providing unequal benefit or punishment to subordinates due to favoritism or non-work-related criteria.
- **Cruelty:** Harming subordinates/colleagues in normally illegitimate ways, such as public humiliation, personal attack, or name-calling.
- **Disregard:** Behaving in ways that violate ordinary standards of politeness and fairness, as well as displaying a flagrant lack of concern for subordinates' lives (e.g., "I do not give a damn about your family's problems.").
- **Deification:** Implying a master-servant status in which bosses can do or say whatever they please to subordinates because they feel themselves to be superior people.

If you have never had a bad boss or worked/lived with difficult colleagues, count yourself blessed. Bosses, who lose their temper, play favorites or cannot communicate—and that is just a start on the list of managerial misbehavior—can make going in to work annoying, humiliating and infuriating. And, unless you are independently wealthy, you are probably not in a position to tell your boss to take this job and forget it. What can you do if you get a boss who is the biggest obstacle to doing—and enjoying—your job or life? You will need a strategy for dealing with the things that your colleagues or boss does or does not do that drive you crazy. A survey carried out by ABC News discovered three biggest sources of conflict at work. These are: conflicts between people of different sexes account for 19 percent of conflicts at work; conflicts between people of different ages, 27 percent and conflicts between people at different levels in the organization, 53 percent.[2]

One strategy that people have always advocated, is give your boss or colleagues a fight when your complaints of verbal harassment by coworkers and supervisors are ignored by management, for example when you are passed over for a promotion in favour of a colleague involved with the boss. Whatever your case, when you pitch battle with your boss or colleagues in league with your boss, there may be snares, bobby traps, and pitfalls your employers or boss can use to oppress and otherwise shatter your life at work. Therefore **to survive in a hostile environment, do not lay hands on the anointed.**

You might be inundated with new names, faces, and responsibilities. By "the anointed" I mean persons in positions of authority, power, decision making or those who have the favour and pleasure of those who are in the corridors of power. The most important name and face belongs to your boss, and your most important responsibility is to please him or her.

Choose the path of peaceful diplomacy. It has been said that diplomacy is the art of thinking twice before saying nothing.[3] But how can you possibly act diplomatically when you have just been unjustly treated, abused, assaulted, maligned and discredited in a place that you both love and depend on for friends, income, and emotional support? While one certainly appreciates the psychological urge to tell-off your supervisor, board of directors, and all company shareholders alike, you can best handle such a hostile environment with personal diplomacy that has an emotional anchor.

Do not kick and scream your way out of the workplace or office of the boss. While it may be entirely understandable that you are boiling and your adrenaline level is high, remember that you will shortly be faced with issues of welfare packages, job terms and even promotions with these same people you are currently telling off, and thereby inciting them to lower your pay, recommendation and promotion. When an administrative conflict arises, they might just leave you to fight your way through the administrative bottle-necks.

Furthermore, your verbal threats of harassment and intimidation may lead to criminal prosecution in addition to your current job or emotional worries that has just begun. In fits of rage, anger and aggression, you can say anything that makes you worthy of prosecution without realizing the consequence. Since these people are in power and authority they can get away with wrongful dismissal damages, charge you for slander to your boss, rope you into theft of office supplies, and/or sabotage of the workplace.

Do not sign anything whatsoever with anybody. While it is true that there are so many persons who are under pressure and suffering in a hostile environment that can agitate for mass petition. Be wary of mob or crowd actions. Most of these persons engaged in the petition, if not all, have a plan B to which you have not been inducted if the petition fails. Your signing a letter of protest or petition puts your job and life on the line and may very well disqualify you from any entitlements whatsoever. Meanwhile, any limited package offered to you on the spot of signing will generally implicate you in the months or years ahead. What happens where that boss is only cautioned and not removed, transferred and his or her appointment not terminated? You have to live with the devil for as long as you remain in that company.

Know that your life does not end with that job or place. When one door closes, another door opens - but we often look so long and so regretfully upon the closed door that we do not see the one which has opened for us. Landing a new employment will provide you with potential windfall monies in addition to new opportunities to exhibit your potentials. The place where you are is still not the best you can be. Therefore, know that your boss does not determine how much your life will progress. The place where you are might be limiting you, do not just get lost in your emotions, you have a lifter. The El-Shaddai, the God with two breast; He can and does care for you. Since you have a future there is no need to get bugged and weighed down with an environment that does not fulfill you: wait it out. Do not be in a hurry: wait out the queries, wait out the abuses, wait out the demonic strategies, wait out the gang ups, and wait out the negative office politics. Its going to happen because you are there to be crowned.

Choose the path of professional discipline. Take a "hands-off" approach: David knew the wisdom in "hands off" approach by not touching the person of Saul because that would have meant touching the power and person behind the throne: the Lord of Israel. In many technical or confidential positions we are privy to a wide variety of sensitive information, sometimes as subordinates. This can include everything from supervisor passwords to file servers, IDs to access high security areas and human resources information on everyone in the company. One of the first things to do when you are in a hostile work environment is distance yourself from any sensitive information or locations that you might find appropriate to implicate your harassers. This is especially true if you are having problems with your employer. In some extreme cases, employers have created problems and tried to blame them on the employee. This is an extreme case but it has happened. Even if your resignation is taken well, you want to insure that there is no way you can be blamed for mishaps that might take place during your last two weeks. If your resignation is contentious you will want to protect yourself from any action, up to and including, litigation. While some of us might consider this an over-reaction, we only need to read the newspapers to see just how nasty the work environment can be.

Keep your mouth shut: David knew that Saul was occasionally acted upon by an unclean spirit, but he shut his mouth up. David never used the secret he knew about Saul to deride him and make him loose his royal image before his subjects. Despite the fact that you may be feeling very unhappy, even exasperated, about your job and life, it is best to contain your frustration in front of all but your most trusted co-workers. Although it may seem obvious, do not make disparaging comparisons between your boss and others. You may be accused of stirring up trouble and, in the worst case, of trying to raise or foment troubles for your co-workers or your new boss. This may seem like an extreme position but some co-workers may feel jealous of your new job and supervisors may feel you are undermining their authority somehow.

Too often we are determined to settle old scores when we finally have found a way to deal with our colleagues or bad bosses and are ready to resign. Do not make a point of telling everyone exactly what you think of them. You must not be in the habit of letting people know how right we are and how wrong they are. Sometimes it seems we want to do as much damage as possible before we leave a place or the more we remain in the place, the more we want to destroy it. In truth, we do more damage to ourselves than the companies or people we are exposing. Engaging in petty reprisals only makes our lives more difficult. When you begin the war, they might hold up your paycheck, dispute your unused vacation, car loan, office grants, imprest, or other official responsibilities. You will find that it is best to let the sins of the past be forgotten, release your anger towards them in a positive way and move on. It is not worth the energy to fight battles that you cannot win, even when you tell off everyone in the company. Direct that energy towards your improvement. Just shut up!⁴

Learn to be a professional and maintain professional ethics. David kept to the oath of the palace not to harm the King he was chosen to serve. Again, he saw a military Saul who was unprotected and in line with custom did not kill a soldier who did not pose any immediate harm to him. In modern society the threats of daily life have taken a different form but they get the same response. Sometimes you are at work when your boss comes and says to you, "Look, that report you did last week has a lot of errors in it. You need to correct it immediately before the staff meeting." As your boss walks off down the hallway you may notice several things happening in your body. You may feel the "butterflies in the belly" sensation as your stomach tightens up. The pounding in your chest becomes noticeable, and you feel your muscles tighten. Your body is sending you an important message. Right at this moment your body is saying that the best course of action is for you to either punch out your supervisor on the spot or to just run screaming down the hall, the door, and all the way home. Your body has prepared you for a fight or flight response. Keep this motto: "Always be a professional despite the provocation." *"Work is one of the most fundamental aspects in a person's life, providing the individual with a means of financial support and, as importantly, a contributory role in society. A person's employment is an essential component of his or her sense of identity, self-worth and emotional well-being."*[5]

In "Men of Honour," a George Tilman Jr., film starring Robert De Niro and Cuba Golding Jr., the story of Carl Brasher epitomizes professional ethics and discipline in a hostile environment. Carl Brasher was the first black navy deep sea diver retriever. During one of the training sessions a bomb exploded which would have killed one of his colleagues. He took a risk and saved the fellow, but because he was black the honour was given to a white colleague. In another incident, during the final stages of training, each student would be given a bag of tools lowered down to fix a problem under water. The tool bag of Carl Brasher was cut open by his white supervisor which made all his tools scatter on the sea floor 1800 feet. Carl Brasher searched and picked out all his tools and fixed his assignment spending eighteen hours in the process under water. Though the action of his white supervisor was intended to make him fail his finals, it became a fit no one had ever achieved in the navy school. Carl Brasher keep his cool, focused on his assignment and graduated. You can gain a lot when you maintain professional discipline and shun local battles.

Everyone wants to know how to get along with a boss, but no one actually wants to do it. Getting along with a boss, even a good one, requires accommodation, acceptance and adjustment. Some people understand this. However, they also cling to the fallacy that getting along with the boss centers on the boss becoming enlightened and changing. That is not likely to happen. The effort to achieve compatibility with the boss may not involve the boss at all. In the real world, workers are the ones who have to do the accommodating, accepting and adjusting, not the boss. This is how it works in business. You can proselytize about how it should be, stand on the principle of fairness, and by default maintain the status quo; or you can personally take the initiative to make your relationship with your boss better. Start by building a strong foundation for a relationship with any boss through your emotional discipline.

Identify the true source of your conflict. Unfortunately, a strained relationship with your boss is not good for your job security. In modern society most of the stressors that create threats are not things that we can actually fight or escape. Most modern stress comes from a variety of psycho/social/emotional events. This means that job stress comes from the social context in which we live and the psychological and emotional reactions to that context. It has been estimated that only about 10% or less of modern stress comes from actual physical threat to life. The other 90% comes from the perception of life events or circumstances. Such sources of stress are financial worries, job conflict, aging parents, children having trouble in school, health problems, crime, and so on. These problems do not easily go away and are hard to fight against. You cannot run away from them and often take them wherever you go. Unknowingly, in reacting to your boss or fellow colleagues these stressors take over your already charged emotions. It is better then to learn to be calm to discover if your boss or colleagues' action was actually enough to have provoked you.

Choose the path of positive dialogue. David knew he was anointed to be King, but he had to wait. When he had the opportunity to kill Saul and finally take care of the threat against his life, he rather opted for dialogue. Force has never solved any problem in the work place. Saul as king had all the resources and state power to take of David. David knew that it would be suicidal to try to engage Saul in open battle; he opted for dialogue with Saul. Before confronting your boss, it is important to decide if the fight is worthwhile by examining the bigger picture and questioning the company or institution as a whole. You can examine if your energy would be better utilized somewhere else, or on something else. For instance, it is a waste of time to battle a boss who has been "demoralized and crushed by your corporation" - he or she will likely move on, sacked, or be replaced by another boss. "You are best to decide if the company is right for you, or if you should be fighting the corporate culture instead" says Jonah c. Nader.[6]

Do not go into any battle with your boss that you cannot win. In fact, it is more advisable to avoid confrontation. You might win the war but you will lose the battle. There are people who are powerful because the boss is the boss; there are people who are important because of the boss; there are people who are honoured because of the boss and there are people who are financially well off because of the boss. When you touch the boss, you touch all these groups of people. They will all pitch battle against you. The evil of this battle is that you might think you are only in battle against the boss, not knowing that you are in battle against an unseen host. More so, because the boss calls the short around the place and in a position of management with others, management is most likely going to give the boss preference. The other bosses might all seek to rally round their colleague. Choose the battle that you have to fight that you do not have to beg tomorrow. During the reign of Oba Ozolua of the great Benin Empire, there was a palace urchin called Nekihidi. He was born almost at the same time with Oba Ozolua and so disrespected the Oba. Nekihidi stole the royal beads from the palace and gathered several rascals to himself who paid obeisance to him. Oba Ozolua chose to be magnanimous and asked Nekihidi to return the royal beads in spite of the fact that he also had proclaimed himself to be a monarch. When the royal emissaries got to him, Nekihidi asked them to bow and salute his self proclaimed royalty, which the royal messengers refused to do. The royal messengers gave Nekihidi the message of Oba Ozolua to return the royal beads he took from the palace or face the consequences of war. Nekihidi in reply said "tell Ozolua that as the Lion roar, so does the tiger." Oba Ozolua in anger mustered his troops and defeated Nekihidi. Do not start a war you cannot win.

Do not be among the people who fling themselves into no-win job battles. Ask yourself certain questions before doing something foolish. Almost everyone has a job horror story where the only thought was getting out of the company as quickly as possible. While companies exist with hostile atmospheres, it is far more important to leave a job on good terms, if you really want to leave. Even in leaving, the first priority is to remain a professional, regardless of the situation. If a company has already shown itself to be less than ideal for you, it will be wise to not add any fuel to fire. In deciding when to fight and when not to fight, here are questions to ask yourself: How much difference does this problem really make in my job life? Is it permanent or transitory? Is it worth possibly making an enemy or enemies? And, most importantly, is there a realistic chance of winning? Know when to fight. There are nervous times to be talking or pressing your case around in a hostile work environment. The words "recession, down sizing and right sizing" are being used more frequently; more companies and institutions are announcing layoffs and job security is suddenly a major concern. Yet you probably have been working more, and know that your performance and results exceed what should be expected of you to keep your job. Should you stay mum? Yes, silence is golden sometimes.

Defer your war to another day: Be gracious and defer battle when there is conflict. Even when you do not think that your boss knows more than you do, she/he probably does. Learn something from experience. Why fight a battle you cannot win? When you get into a fight you sink to the level of your harassers. Because that is their world, thy fight dirty. Can you? You might not win them all. Even Andry Schevchenko, Roberto

Baggio, J.J. Okocha, Kano Nwankwo, Samuel Etoo, Socrates, Micelle Platini Zico ,Didier Drogba, Lionel Messi, and Christiano Ronaldo - great footballers in their right - have all missed goals and did not get passes across about 65% of the time, yet, they carried on. When you know that lose sometimes does not end your story, you would not squander your energy, the goodwill of your allies, and the patience of your boss by turning every issue into a personal crusade. Perhaps the best long-term strategy is to put the ball in your boss's court by asking questions. "What would it take for me to get the best that you desire"? If your boss can explain what the rules are, you can tailor your ongoing behavior to qualify. If you use this strategy, do not be afraid to be clear about exactly what you want.

Your boss might be a pain in your neck, but be careful before picking a fight with him/her. Before you challenge your boss, always do your homework. Ask, could I be wrong? What proof do I have that supports my current position? How can it be argued out? Know that everyone gets upset about stupid stuffs done by the boss and the other executives and you cannot be an exception. But then remember that in spite of their "stupid stuffs", they call the shots. So, learn that rather than going around with a bad attitude, you just have to approach your job like it is a job, you have to accept that other people are in a position to tell you what to do. Ever since I accepted that, being in leadership position as a pastor, people are going to hurt me knowingly or unknowingly, my job has been much more bearable.

Come to terms with boss power. The fact remains that the boss has the power and you do not. This is reality. When you are the boss you will have the power (and the responsibility and the accountability, etc.), but until then you have to acknowledge that someone else is in charge and you are not. Without accepting this you will not be successful with your boss. Recognize that the relationship is your responsibility. Do not presume that the boss has the responsibility to get along with you. That is not true. You are responsible for getting along with the boss. Look to yourself when there are problems. Even if you are not at fault you are likely to have to solve it or live with it. It is in accepting the boss's power you control your emotions. Sit down to ask yourself soul searching questions: Is the boss being totally unreasonable, or are her/his decisions, or her/his style, just not to my liking? Regardless, she/he is still the boss. Negativity is useless to you. It is possible that there are considerations of which you are unaware that affect decisions you dislike. Your attitude towards the boss may be a big part of the relationship problem. It is your responsibility to have a good attitude, regardless of the boss's attitude.

Learn the act of negotiation. Stay cool under pressure; stand up for yourself without provoking opposition; deal with underhanded tactics; find mutually agreeable options and then move on. Negotiations can be formal or informal, but it must be done without humiliating or destroying the other side. Phrase everything as a win-win. Do not walk into your boss's office, throw a hiss, or fist and say that you need new furniture *NOW!* That is negative style. Whenever possible, explain your ideas in terms of how they would benefit the other person, not how they would benefit you. Tend to be more sympathetic with their position since accountability rests with them. Forget about yourself sometimes. You have to make bosses understand why you want them to do what you want them to do. Once, the boss can positively position himself/herself in the picture, the matter is solved.

Extend the benefit of the doubt to your boss. You do not know all the facts associated with your company, work or hostility. Give a boss the benefit of the doubt even in your hostile environment. It really costs you nothing but the effort to do so. Lend support to the difficult boss and evil colleagues. Extend a kind word of encouragement, acknowledgement, or appreciation. Bosses are people. Admittedly, they are people with power, but people nonetheless. Not every positive exchange between a boss and a worker has to be brown-nosing. Bosses rarely, if ever, receive positive feedback from workers. Think about how much better you do your own work when you feel appreciated.

Accept the boss's attitude. You are not likely to effect any meaningful change in the boss's attitude if your attitude remains negative. If you like the job, except for the boss, then accept what you cannot change: the boss. Put the boss's attitude in perspective and choose not to be annoyed or upset by it.[7] Highlight the positives of the job, rather than the negatives of the boss. You have the power to do this. Sometimes, just because we do not personally like a co-worker or boss does not mean that we cannot learn from their opinions, viewpoints and ideas. If we can find something to appreciate about them, comment on it in a favourable way. If that person senses our allegiance, they will be naturally drawn to us and we may both learn to get along despite our differences.

Remember, if you cannot avoid a hostile environment, you can advance in it. What you feed into the environment determines what it becomes for you. If you must live, work or learn in a place with other colleagues and a boss, determine to survive. You have all the survival tools in you. Make it happen! Peace to your heart.

END NOTES

PREFACE.

1. T. D. Jakes, *Ten Commandments of Working in a Hostile Environment*, (New York: Berkley Publishing Group, 2005).

CHAPTER ONE.

1. http://counsel.wlu.edu/tutorial/cair&do.discrimharass.2005.ppt.
2. http://www.bambooweb.com/articles/h/a/Harassment.html
3. Rick Meyers, *E-Sword Electronic online ver*sion, 2005.
4. Rick Meyers, *E-Sword Electronic online ver*sion, 2005.
5. http://www.timslaw.com/retaliation.html
6. This reminds me of the novel by S.M.O. Aka, *My Father's car is Bigger than Yours*. (Benin City: S.M.O Aka press).
7. Rick Meyers, *E-Sword Electronic online ver*sion, 2005.
8. http://www.timslaw.com/sexual-harassment.html

CHAPTER TWO.

1. http://www.bambooweb.com/articles/h/a/Harassment.html
2. Cardinal Newman., *Grammar of Assent*, 112 quoted in http://www.newmanreader.org/biography/ward/volume2/workindex2.html

CHAPTER THREE

1. Rick Meyers, *E-Sword Electronic online ver*sion, 2005.
2. http://www.wisdomquotes.com/002094.html
3. http://www.wisdomquotes.com/002094.html

CHAPTER FOUR

1. The personality types are many depending on how an author perceives them. They types 1 have mentioned fit into my own perspective. However, there are many others which appear obvious though not cited by me. See the following sources for a discussion of various personality types and how to handle them. http://www.askmen.com/money/career_100/122b_career.html, http://www.theconsultingteam.com/ http://www.confidencecenter.com/ free.htm and Gini Graham Scott, *A Survival Guide for Working with Humans: Dealing with Whiners, Back-Stabbers, Know-It-Alls, and Other Difficult People.*

2. Elwood N. Chapman, *Attitude: Your Most Priceless Possession.*
3. BBC News, 12th September 2004.
4. Erik Giltay Institute of Mental Health in Deft, the Netherlands.
5. Anthony Robbins , Awaken *the Giant Within,* (New York: Summit Books, 1991).
6. http://www.apa.org/topics/controlanger.html
7. http://www.apa.org/topics/controlanger.html

CHAPTER FIVE.

1. Andrew DuBrin, *Winning Office Politics,* (New Jersey: Prentice Hall, 1990).
2. I lost the source of this information. There was not deliberate action to omit it.
3. Andrew DuBrin, *Winning Office Politics,*
4. Alesko, Michael. "Office Politics: Do You Play or Pass," *Today's Careers,* quoted in http://www.123oye.com/job-articles/office/workplace-politics.htm
5. See "Surviving Office Politics." *Talent Scout,* April 16, 1998 qouted in http://careerplanning.about.com/od/workplacesurvival/a/politics.htm
6. Erin Burt , "Seven Career Killers," cited by Jo Miller, "How Smart Women win at Office politics" in http://www.careerknowhow.com/
7. Matthew 22:21. "They said to Him, "Caesar's." And He said to them, "Render therefore to Caesar the things that are Caesar's, and to God the things that are God's."
8. Quoted by Aleksandra Todorova, "Oh, Boy. An Office Party, Mind These Do's and Don'ts," in http://www.careerjournal.com/myc/officelife/ 20051220-todorova.html
9. See Nkrumah Steward, "Office Politics: How I Get Fucked At My Job, in "http://www.eightballmagazine.com/subculture/contact.htm
10. http://www.workingwounded.com/
11. For various articles and discussion of details on the games, do's and don'ts of office politics with its accompanying results see http://www.ivillage.co.uk/workcareer/survive/archive/0,,156475,00.html
12. Adrian W. Savage, "The Laws of Executive Politics, (1)" posted on July 19, 2005 in http://www.adriansavage.com/blog/OfficePolitics/ _ archives/2005/7/20/1054963.html
13. See "Prevent Office Politics From Ruining Your Career", in http://www.hypnosisnetwork.com/index.php
14. Susan Donaldson James, "How to survive office politics and power struggles," in *Careers,* Friday, December 30, 2005, http://www.detnews.

com/ apps/pbcs.dll/article?AID=/20051230/BIZ02/51229020/1010/
BIZ&template=printart

15. Marty Nemko, "win at office politics without selling your soul," in
    http://wlb.monster.com/

16. Mohan Babu, "Navigating office politics," in http://www.garamchai.com/
    index.html

CHAPTER SIX

1. Beverley Kaye, *Up is Not the Only Way*, 1987 cited by Mike Keelen,
   "Development Through Mentoring," http://www.sportrec.qld.gov.
   au/ zone_files/Industry_information/stream_2__session_3_-_mike_
   keelan.ppt

2. WWWebster Dictionary. See also http://www.wordreference.com/
   definition/mentor , and http://www.yourdictionary.com/ahd/m/m 022
   23 00.html

3. www.mtrohealth.org/clinical/anes/mentor.aspBelow are definitions of
   who a mentor is collected by Andrew Gibbons:

   1. "Mentoring is a long term relationship that meets a development
       need, helps develop full potential, and benefits all partners,
       mentor, mentee and the organization". - Suzanne Faure

   2. "Mentoring is a protected relationship in which learning and
       experimentation can occur, potential skills can be developed,
       and in which results can be measured in terms of competencies
       gained". - Audrey Collin

   3. Mentoring is "A mutual relationship with an intentional
       agenda designed to convey specific content along with life
       wisdom from one individual to another. Mentoring does not
       happen by accident, nor do its benefits come quickly. It is
       relationally based, but it is more than a good friendship…
       mentoring is not two people who just spend time together
       sharing". - Thomas Addington and Stephen Graves

   4. "Mentoring is a supportive learning relationship between
       a caring individual who shares knowledge, experience and
       wisdom with another individual who is ready and willing
       to benefit from this exchange, to enrich their professional
       journey". - Suzanne Faure

   5. "Mentoring is an important adult relationship since it creates
       a legitimate and special space where people can take chances

by trying to be authentic about, and find meaning within their real-life professional experience". - D Doyon

6. "The purpose of mentoring is always to help the mentee to change something - to improve their performance, to develop their leadership qualities, to develop their partnership skills, to realize their vision, or whatever. This movement from where they are, ('here'), to where they want to be ('there'). - Mike Turner

7. "Mentoring involves primarily listening with empathy, sharing experience (usually mutually), professional friendship, developing insight through reflection, being a sounding board, encouraging" - David Clutterbuck

8. "Mentoring is an intense work relationship between senior and junior organizational members. The mentor has experience and power in the organization, and personally advises, counsels, coaches and promotes the career development of the protégé" - Anne Stockdale …and thoughts on what it takes to be a mentor

9. A mentor is…"an accomplished and experienced performer who takes a special, personal interest in helping to guide and develop a junior or more inexperienced person". - Stephen Gibb

10. "A mentor should have the qualities of experience, perspective and distance, challenging the mentee and using candour to force re-examination and reprioritization without being a crutch". - Christopher Conway

11. "A mentor facilitates personal and professional growth in an individual by sharing the knowledge and insights that have been learned through the years. The desire to want to share these 'life experiences' is characteristic of a successful mentor". - Arizona National Guard

12. "Mentors in the workplace are simply people who help other people succeed". - Neave Hospital Southern Minnesota

13. "A mentor is a more experienced individual willing to share knowledge with someone less experienced in a relationship of mutual trust" - David Clutterbuck

14. A mentor is…"A trusted counsellor or guide. Normally a senior person to the associate. A mentor is a counsellor, coach, motivator, and role model. A mentor is a person who has a

sincere desire to enhance the success of others. A person who volunteers time to help the associate". - Air National Guard USA

15. "A mentor is someone who can patiently assist with someone's growth and development in a given area. This assistance can come in the form of guidance, teaching, imparting of wisdom and experience". - Chicago Computer Society

16. "A great mentor has a knack for making us think we are better than we think we are. They force us to have a good opinion of ourselves, let us know they believe in us. They make us get more out of ourselves, and once we learn how good we really are, we never settle for anything less than our very best". - The Prometheus Foundation. http://www.coachingnetwork.org. uk/resourcecentre/Articles/ View Article.asp?artId=54

4. Smith, R. & Alfred, G. "The impersonation of wisdom," In *Mentoring perspectives on school-based teacher education,* Edited by D. McIntyre, H. Hagger, & M. Wilkin, (London: Kogan, 1994), 103-106.

5. J. Mallison, "Who nurtures our leaders?" *Alive Magazine*, April, 2002, 26-30.

6. Lawrie, 1998, 4.

7. "Surviving Office Politics," http://www.chiff.com/

8. For a discussion of research and results see James B. Rowley, "The Good Mentor," In *Educational Leadership,* Volume 56, Number 8, May 1999, 20-22.

9. For a discussion of how to find a good mentor see the following sources: http://apps.mentoring.org/training/TMT/tmt20010.adp, http://www.learnthat.com/define/mentor.asp, http://www.imdiversity. com/ Villages/Careers/articles/edward_jones_052004b.asp and http://www.humanresourcesmagazine.com.au/article_sendtofriend. asp?articleid=201583255,

10. Proverbs 27:17. "As iron sharpens iron, so a man sharpens the countenance of his friend."

11. Rick Meyers, *E-Sword Electronic online ver*sion, 2005.

12. Rick Meyers, *E-Sword Electronic online ver*sion, 2005.

13. http://www.nightingale.com/tAE_Article~ArticleID~160~Page~1. asp

14. T. Lasley, "Mentors: They simply believe," *Peabody Journal of Education,*(1), 71, 1996, 64–70)

15. http://www.umich.edu/~mcgrads/Character/Character_Page.htm

16. http://www.coachingnetwork.org.uk/resourcecentre/Articles/ViewArticle.asp?artId=54

17. http://uk.mf.sports.yahoo.com/mailto?url=http%3A%2F%2Fuk.sports.yahoo.com%2F04052006%2F3%2Fearl-woods-tiger-s-father-guiding-mentor-dies-cancer.html&title=Earl%20Woods%2C%20Tiger's%20father%20and%20 guiding%20mentor%2C%20dies%20of%20cancer&locale=uk&prop=sport&h2=899425

18. Bob Shank cited in D. Otto, *Finding a mentor, being a mentor,* (Oregon: Harvest House, 2001), 17.

19. Consult the resources in end note 9 for guidance in finding a suitable mentor.

20. Dawn Rosenberg McKay, "Why You Should Have A Mentor," http://clk.about.com/?zi=18/15t&sdn=careers_careerplanning&tm=4&gps=393_10_979_605&f=00&su=p496.9.140.ip_p554.1.150.ip_p560.1.150.ip_p284.1.420.ip_&tt=2&bt=0&bts=0&zu=http%3A//careerplanning.about.com/od/workplacesurvival/

21.   Ellen A. Fagenson, "The Mentor Advantage: Perceived Career/Job Experiences of Proteges Versus Non-Proteges," *Journal of Organizational Behavior*, Vol. 10, No. 4. (Oct., 1989), 309-320 and Katharine Hansen, "The Value of a Mentor, http://www.quintcareers.com /printable/mentor_value.html

CHAPTER SEVEN

1. Eric Parsloe, *The Manager as Coach and Mentor*, 2nd Edition, (London:CIPD Enterprises Limited, 1999), 8. See also Eric Parsloe & Monika Wray, *Coaching & Mentoring*, (Kogan 2000).

2. See http://www.mentalgamecoach.com/Services/ExecutiveCoaching.html and http://www.archaeologists.net/modules/icontent/inPages/docs/ training/en_mentor_manual.pdf.

3. See http://www.1to1coachingschool.com/Courses_for_license.htm

4. Eric Parsloe, *The Manager as Coach and Mentor* (1999), 8.

5. Quoting Ronald Burt, http://www.ggci.com/blog/archive/2004_05_01_archive.htm

6. Byron & Catherine Pulsifer, "Goodbye Manager, Hello Coach," http://www.wow4u.com/hellocommon2/index.html

7. Gallwey, Timothy, *The Inner Game of Tennis,* (New York: Random House, inc., 1974).

8. Walter Rychlewski, "Roles and Qualities of a Mentor**,**" http://www.kcsmallbiz.com/may-2005/ http://www.direct.gov.uk/ExternalLink?

EXTERNAL_LINK=http%3A//www. coachingnetwork.org.uk/ ResourceCentre/WhatAreCoachingAndMentoring.htm and http:// www.coachingnetwork.org.uk/ResourceCentre/WhatAreCoaching AndMentoring.htm

9. Eric, Parsloe, *Coaching, Mentoring and Assessing,*
10. *Daily Sun,* June 4, 2006, 37.
11. Stephen Bangert, "Advantages of a Career Coach," in http://www. wsacorp.com/articles/PrintOut/FATadvantagesCoach.htm
12. Bill Altreuter, "Qualities of a Good Coach," http://www.typepad.com/ t/trackback/4661743 April 13, 2006. See also Peters, T. & Austin, N., *A passion for excellence,* (Random House, New York, 1985).
13. http://www.biotactics.com/Celebrus/celebruscoach.htm
14. Robert, Quinn, et al., *Becoming a Master Manager,* (John Wiley and Sons, 1996)
15. http://www.ggci.com/executive-coaching/

CHAPTER EIGHT.

1. wordnet.princeton.edu/perl/webwn
2. http://www.answers.com/topic/integrity-unity-wholeness, and http:// en.wikipedia.org/wiki/Integrity
3. Cheshire, Calhoun, 'Standing for Something.' *Journal of Philosophy* XCII, 1995, 235-260.
4. Calhoun, 258.
5. *Human Resource Magazine,* May, 2006, in http://www.findarticles /p/ articlesmi_m3495
6. http://www.kfmb.com/features/special_assignment/story.php?id= 42030%5C
7. Kate DuBose Tomassi, http://www.wired.com/news/culture/0,71047-0. html, http://www.forbes.com/2006/05/20/resume-lies-work_cx_ kdt_ 06work_0523lies.html , and http://www.finance.news.com.au/ story/0,10166, 19315804-462,00.html
8. Sissela Bok, *Lying: Moral Choice in Public and Private Life,* (New York' Pantheon. 1978). According to a review on http://www.florin. com /authors/bok-lying.html "Bok examines the effects of lying and deception upon society and individuals, challenging the reader to consider any justifications that might exist for this pervasive practice. This book guides us through a journey fraught with moral and ethical questions, covering a full spectrum from white lies to those that might be necessary for survival when faced with serious dangers. In

questioning whether any degree of lying can be justified, Bok provides many examples from daily life to illustrate the perspectives of both the liar and the deceived." Addressing the power of lying in modern society, this book stimulates the reader into becoming more aware of its consequences for social behaviour. By using a philosophical approach with contrasting opinions and beliefs, Bok offers some refreshing insights intended to enable the reader to resolve the associated ethical dilemma."

9. http://www.spectacle.org/0500/lies.html .
10. http://www.guidetopsychology.com/honesty.htm
11. en.wikipedia.org/wiki/Instinct.
12. www.willdurant.com/glossary.htm

CHAPTER NINE.

1. Steve Fraser, http://www.tothenextlevel.org/docs/ mental_skills/ training_mental_toughness.html
2. Rick Meyers, *E-Sword*.
3. http://en.wikipedia.org/wiki/Camouflage_(disambiguation)
4. http://en.wikipedia.org/wiki/Camouflage_(disambiguation)
5. http://www.wellingtonzoo.com/learn/teacher/camouflage.html
6. CHAPTER TEN.
7. http://www.itstime.com/apr97.htm
8. A survey published in *New York Times,* January 17, 1989
9. *Science,* June 19, 1988.
10. Koffi Annan quoted by Luul Yehdego, "Strong family bonds, a sine qua non for national and regional cohesion," in http://www.unmeeonline. org /index.php?option=com_content&task=view&id=343&Itemid=8 5
11. http://www.acf.hhs.gov/programs/family_celebration.htm
12. http://www.acf.hhs.gov/programs/family_celebration.htm
13. http://www.acf.hhs.gov/programs/family_celebration.htm
14. Jerome Fleg quoted by http://www.ediets.com/news/article.cfm? cmi=1207066&cid=28 and http://www.lifescript.com/channels/well_ being/ Inspiration/the_power_of_laughter.asp
15. Bernie Siegel, cited by John H. Sklare, "The Power of Laughter for Health," *Life Script,* February 8, 2006, http://www.lifescript.com/ channels/ well_being/Inspiration/the_power_of_laughter.asp
16. 10 Paul E. McGhee, "Humor and Health, cited by John H. Sklare, "Laughter: Medicine for good Health," *Diet and Nutrition,* http://

www.ediets.com/news/article.cfm/2/cmi_1207066/cid_28/ and http://www.lifescript.com/channels/well_being/Inspiration/the_power_of_laughter.asp

17. Beverly Brummett, http://www.lifescript.com/channels/well_being / Inspiration/the_power_of_laughter.asp

18. http://www.oprah.com/spiritself/lybl/well/ss_lybl_well_health04_e.jhtml

19. See http://www.laughteryoga.org/research.php, and http://www.thisisawar.com/LaughterHealing.htm,

20. http://www.backandneck.about.com/mbiopage.htm http://www.phillyburbs.com/pb-dyn/news/94-03082004-260503.html and http://www.americanscientist.org/template/AssetDetail/assetid/24591?fulltext=true&print=yes

21. J., Rispens, J.M.A. Hermanns, & W.H.J. Meeus, (Eds. *Opvoeden in Nederland*, (Assen: Van Gorcum, 1996)

22. G. Kronjee, Veranderingen in de levenscyclus, demografische veroudering en collectieve sociale uitgaven, (Dissertatie Rijksuniversiteit Utrecht, 1991).

23. M.E. Lamb, J.H. Pleck & J.A. Levine. "The role of the father in child development," in *Advances in clinical child psychology 8*, Edited by B.B. Lahey & A.E. Kazdin, (New York: Plenum, 1985), 229-266.

24. M, Kalmijn, "Father Involvement in childrearing and the perceived stability of marriage," *Journal of Marriage and the Family*, 61, 1999, 409-421.

25. M, Du Bois-Reymond, "'I don't want to commit myself yet': Young people's life concepts," *Journal of Youth Studies, 1*, 1998, 63-79.

26. P.A. Dykstra, "The effects of divorce on intergenerational exchanges in families," *The Netherlands Journal of Social Sciences, 33*, 1993, 77-93.

27. Rick Meyers, *E-Sword*.

28. Byrne & Kelley, in http://www.mentalhelp.net/poc/view_doc.php?type=doc&id=9852&cn=353

29. Aronson, 1984; Berkowitz, 1989

30. http://mhnet.org/psyhelp/chap7/chap7d.htm

31. http://www.aish.com/spirituality/48ways/Way_22_Conquer_Frustration.asp

32. http://www.nlpjerusalem.com/DisplayArticle.asp?ID=24

CHAPTER ELEVEN.

1. See Henry Blackaby and Claude King, *Experiencing God.*

2. http://www.horizonsnet.org/sermons/sermons.html

CHAPTER TWELVE.

1. http://www.asianexec.com/asp/tellarticle.asp?title=Feeling%20 abused%20at%20the%20workplace?
2. http://abcnews.go.com/Business/WorkingWounded/
3. See Attorney Howard Markowitz , http://64.177.126.252/emotional_ strategy.html
4. Pastor John Haggi of Cornerstone Church, San Antonio, Texas, U.S.A., in his message "Favour" noted also that some of us bring attacks to ourselves because we have not learnt to shut up. He said Joseph in Genesis 37 told everyone about his destiny dream and that became the path to several troubles.
5. Chief Justice Dickson, in *Reference re: Public Service Employee Relations Act* (Alberta: 1987), 1 S.C.R. 313 (Supreme Court of Canada), 368 cited by Attorney Howard Markowitz , in " http://64.177.126.252/ emotional_ strategy.html
6. Jonar C. Nader, "Five Tips for being Assertive with your boss," http:// superperformance.com/articles.html
7. Sloan Fader, "What Your Boss Wants You to Know," *The Demotech Difference*, volume 1, Issue 8 , December 28, 2004. http://www. pulpfusion1.com/demotech/index000069012.cfm?x=b11,0,w

While we seek to overcome the hostile work, living or learning environment it is necessary to inform you that there is a hostile environment which will last for eternity. That environment is called "Hell fire" where Satan and all who reject the Lordship of Jesus Christ would remain forever.

You can however overcome that hostile environment when you make Jesus Lord and Saviour over your life now. It is quite simple. Just pray and say: "Lord Jesus, I believe that you came to this world, you died, rose and would come again. Please forgive me my sins and come into my heart as Lord and Saviour. Cancel my name from the book of death and write my name in the book of life."

If you said that prayer consciously and meant it, you have just become saved and a citizen of heaven. Join a Bible believing Church and live for God.

You can reach the author through any of the following addresses:

Living Oracles Ministry,
% Covenant Life Baptist Church,
15 Lucky Agbonsevbafe Street,
E.D.P.A Estate, opposite U.B.T.H,
P.O. Box 4024, Benin City, Nigeria.
Website: www.livingoracles.net
Email: pasceedee@yahoo.ca, cceedee@excite.com or chika@livingoracles.net

ABOUT THE BOOK

In an increasingly competitive world where each environment for work, learning or living tends to provoke hostility and mutual suspicion among colleagues and between subordinates, *Survival in a Hostile Environment* comes as a most welcome handbook and manual.

Almost everyone that would be considered a "mature adult" has been in a hostile environment or would be in one point of time or another. Thus *survival* is a must-read for those already facing untoward human challenges in their jobs, schools or residences. It is also an asset to those who are yet free from such hostility – to enable them to recognize possible budding signs of hostile environments. The book also commends itself to individuals in positions of authority or leadership – almost everyone dreams to be one some day – to watch their thoughts, words and actions, lest they constitute hostile environments, even if inadvertently, to their followers, staff, students and neighbours.

The greatest strength of *survival* is it success in drawing spiritual lessons and bringing these to bear directly on a practical, topical issue in contemporary society. The clarity of expression, the vividness in illustration and the currency of the real-life data and events used to substantiate the principles make the admonitions authentic and engaging. The author's ability to use religious principles to demonstrate the secular issues of interpersonal conflicts and rivalry in our daily lives makes this book an ecclesiastical treatise and a scholarly thesis fused in one.

Diri I. Teilanyo, PhD
Senior Lecturer,
Department of English and Literature,
University of Benin,
Benin City, Nigeria.

A book that exposes the simple solutions to the seeming difficult and frustrating experiences we encounter in our work environment. After completing the book, you learn to trust in the power deposited in you rather than be swayed by intrigues.

Andrew Otike-Odibi. FCAN
Director,
C & I Holdings,
Port Harcourt, Nigeria.

Most Christians are generally idealists. "I am a child of God" "The Holy Spirit rules over my life, my home, my job/business". In offices, you find inscriptions like, "Christ is in charge here; the Holy Spirit is the Boss". Armed with these assurances, the good Christian deludes himself into thinking that no evil will ever come near him and he therefore conducts his business life as if life is a bed of roses.

In *Survival In A Hostile Environment,* Rev Chika Diokpala Ossai-Ugbah says that this is a most dangerous assumption. He avers that business life is full of political intrigues and that the work place is a proper arena for testing ones ability to survive. In fact, in our work life, we operate in a hostile environment, which at best is concealed, but in most cases open. Success in work life therefore depends to a large extent on faithful acceptance of this truism and the realistic mastery of the principles, which ensure survival in a hostile environment.

Survival In A Hostile Environment anatomizes these principles and teaches the reader to apply them to real life situations. The ease with which the writer uses the story of David as contained in 1 Samuel 18 to 1 Samuel 24 as a vehicle to teach, "People management" in an organizational setting is amazing. I have not come across any other book on this subject matter that favourably compares with this one in details and lucidity.

Everyone (like me) who has had the harrowing experience of working under a hostile boss would wish that he came in contact with this book earlier. But blessed are all who are still in active working life and those who are yet to start if they take this book and read it and apply the principles therein enunciated.

Wilfred O. Mokogwu
Retired Director,
Delta State Library Services,
Asaba, Nigeria.

Survival in a hostile environment (What to Do when your Boss/Colleagues want you Dead) is an intellectual force of the work environment and its challenges as well as the mechanism for transcending the identified challenges. The Saul/David story provided the appropriate biblical backdrop for the tremendous intellectual dissection of this topical issue.

Nobody with some insight into the nuances of the work environment can remain untouched by the invigorating and insightful manner the author explored the main theme of discourse, particularly the survival mechanism so painstakingly provided. It will required some special ingenuity to improve on the author's handling of the subject matter.

Jonathan I. Nikori,
Managing Director,
Inter Arch Consultants Ltd,
Akpakpavba Road, Benin City,
Edo State, Nigeria.

Survival In A Hostile Environment is a that will open the eyes of many to situations that they have accepted cannot be changed. Many of us contend every day with difficult bosses, uncooperative colleagues and enemies who pretend to friends. We are harassed daily and we have accepted this as one of the lots of life.

However, *Survival In A Hostile Environment* opens your eyes to appreciate your environment and all the attending forces. It also teaches you how to manage your environment and be in control rather than succumb. You cannot fail to be what God wants you to be in whatever situation you find yourself after you have read and imbibed all the instructions and admonitions contained therein.

Rev. Ossai-Ugbah, through this book has librated many from the bondage of a hostile work and living environment. The book is educative, incisive, inspiring, and leads you to dare to be a master despite the limitations of your environment. Dare to read it.

Dr. Emmanuel Oghre,
Former Assistant Dean, Faculty of Science,
University of Benin,
Benin City, Nigeria.

Well research, incisive and instructive.

Sym Otike-Odibi. LL.B, BL.
Senior Partner,
Johnson Byrant & Co,
Lagos, Nigeria.

A must for every aspiring graduate who wants to excel in his/her chosen profession.

Solomon Omonigho,
Senior Lecturer,
Department of Micro Biology,
University of Benin,
Benin City, Nigeria.